The
Greatest
Noel

A Fantasy of the First Christmas

A Novel of the Nativity

by

Steve Lawson

CONTENTS

To Evelyn

a true miracle,
a gift every day

AUTHOR'S NOTE

Everyone knows "the Christmas story." Yet while it is the foundation of the most influential and widely-practiced religion in history, the Christmas story remains just that – a story.

Or is it? It is populated with people everybody knows, who really existed, and whom many of us love and have loved from childhood. The Gospel narratives purport to be true reports. Many of us celebrate them annually as such.

So – why is this a "fantasy" of that first Christmas?

Because as familiar as are the accounts from Luke and Matthew, we do not know with certainty what happened – or all that happened – in the hours preceding and following the scene at the manger. Even after researching as much of those days as the evidence allows, Christian and Jewish theologians, historians, anthropologists, archaeologists, and astronomers, and even scholars claiming no religious affiliation, disagree about almost everything.

So I did not feel I was presuming too much to imagine a livelier and more intimate account of that world-changing day and night. The Nativity is already a wonderful story;

I've just hung a few ornaments on it to make it shine a little brighter and nudge the imagination.

While I researched what the world was like around the time of the Nativity to give this tale the feel of its age, I have taken liberties with time, place, character, language, customs – just about everything, including the Gospels' accounts themselves.

In particular, I have conflated certain events in time. Just as coffee-table crèches and Christmas card art combine several Gospel narratives into a Nativity tableau taking place in a single night at a single place, so I have done with my story.

I have also imagined rather different versions of several elements of the Gospel stories, versions that (I nevertheless feel) keep to the spirit and meaning of the verses from Matthew and Luke, and that are consistent with the roles the Bible has assigned to each of the Nativity actors. In a couple of cases, my inventions resolve some of the perplexities people have noticed in those few verses.

My aim has not been to improve on a story that doesn't need improving, or to "correct" the Biblical accounts. Instead, I have tried to weave the events of the Nativity Gospels into a tapestry that compresses into two days and two nights the excitement and wonder experienced by real human beings at a real place at a real time.

I have been honored and humbled to give voice to Mary, Joseph, the Wise Men, the Innkeeper, the Shepherds, and others, having them speak words they never spoke and act in scenes that never took place. I have given each a personality that is entirely invented. I have made up characters who had no role in the Nativity and sent them on a wholly fictional – and wonder-filled – journey to manger-side and on into legend.

With . . . a touch of romance along the way.

Perhaps a laugh or two.

And let's not forget the animals.

But irrespective of the dramatic license I have exercised and the fictional overstory with which I have umbrellaed those hours, it is my hope that this novel will be accepted for what it is:

A fanciful account of events surrounding the birth of Jesus that is respectful of the Nativity's meaning for people of faith, and, for everyone else, of the story they have come to love.

Thank you for accepting this novel on its own terms. I hope it brings you the joy in its reading I felt in its writing.

Steve Lawson
November 2022

A Living Rain

Several months ago . . .

Now in those days no one called him Herod the Great.

This day, he did not feel great, or good, or even satisfactory. He could not bear to sit on his throne while he waited for his official visitor. Its severe angles and stone sides stoked the fire in his groin and kept his aching frame still and rigid as he exercised what kingly governing he was called upon to perform, or that struck his fancy when he was feeling up to issuing a decree or two.

Instead, this day he was reclining on a cushioned *lectus* he had brought back from a visit to Rome. His friend Caesar Augustus – he thought Augustus was his friend, he used to be his friend – had been relaxing on such a couch when Herod had arrived for an audience some months back. He thought it might ease his joints and permit such naps as affairs of state and his searing lap allowed.

No, he did not feel greatness in his bones this day. And his mind was troubled.

He roused himself when the Chief Priest entered the room.

"Where have you been?"

A simple question with some heat to it, best answered simply and promptly. "My cousin was married in Arimathea," the Chief Priest said. "I had been asked to –"

"How was the weather there?"

"Weather, my king?" Herod had never expressed the least curiosity about the weather outside the walls of the palace, much less elsewhere. "Grey skies and a little drizzle, but the wedding feasts –"

"Hmp. A little drizzle."

The Chief Priest waited until he thought it safe to speak again. "My uncle Zalman asked that I convey his res–"

"What did you ride here from Arimathea? A dead ox? It's been over a week since I called for you."

"I started back as soon as I received your summons, my king. I just arrived and came straight here. I was concerned you were unwell."

"I am unwell. I'm always unwell. But I'm not dead yet and do not require your services in ushering me into Sheol."

"My king, I'm certain that in your time you will go to a brighter pl–"

"The captivity."

It was unwise to fail to respond even to Herod's most bewildering utterances. "My king?"

"Our people. Jews. You're one. Remember? One

pharoah or another held us captive hundreds of years. The plagues, God sent plagues. Tell me about the plagues."

The Chief Priest thought that any of the priests of the palace could have told Herod about the plagues of Egypt. It was unnecessary that he be called from his cousin's festivities – the young girls looking forward to their own wedding days languid and enchanting in brilliant garments draped over their unspoiled curves – for the simplest of Torah lessons. His friend Yoram's frisky daughter Leah was almost of age, and she brightened his mind in a moment before his focus returned to the corroding old man before him.

"There were ten," the Chief Priest began. "Moses and Aaron –"

"Yes, yes, ten. Everyone knows, ten plagues."

"My king, I might wish to refresh my recall on each of them before –"

"Begin. We'll call for a text if you need it."

"The first plague was the turning of the waters of Egypt into blood. The scripture –"

"Yes, yes, very famous, the Nile, blood, the stink. What was next?"

"Frogs."

"Stop."

๛

A couple of weeks earlier . . .

The still, the boy Tobias thought. *This quiet is speaking.*

Tobias wiped a drop from his forehead. Then a second,

a big drop, and he knew from the unusual afternoon darkness that trying to stay dry would be useless.

The shepherds usually welcomed the rain. Its visits were irregular but necessary, recharging the streams and ponds where they watered their flocks in the meadows and hills south of Bethlehem. The rains were usually gentle and brief, and the men did little more than cover themselves and let the sheep cool off and smell like wet sheep for a day or two.

This rain was different. The lightning and wind were ferocious; Tobias feared for the small flock the men let him tend. The sheep huddled and cried as the rain stung their naked faces.

Then Tobias saw his father stiffen and stare at the southern sky.

His father Eli was the bravest man he knew, honored among the shepherds for his sense and strength and his few but clear words. But even from a half-field away Tobias could tell that he was seeing something that fixed him to his spot and caused his eyes to open wide.

Tobias heard the howl before he saw the spinning cloud dip from the sky. In all the tales the men had told of the unusual things they had seen in a life spent in the hills, they had never mentioned a whirling sky-spear like this. Its roar was steady, not rumbling or clapping like thunder, growing louder as it approached.

For all its bluster, Tobias could see it was not going to molest the stock. The sinewy shape danced over the countryside to the south, swaying around to the hills east of the flocks, kicking up dust when it felt at the earth, teasingly pretending to recede into its mother cloud before reaching down again. Its violence seemed almost playful.

Then, as if it were having second thoughts about leaving so much rain on the countryside, the funnel began to tap the ponds and marshes. The twister brightened with their waters as its winds spiraled back up into heaven.

What is this? Tobias thought. *What little water God gives us, He's taking back?*

Satisfied with its fun, the skipping cone disappeared into the squall as the storm moved north toward Jerusalem. Tobias watched as his father went from group to group to check on the flocks. He'd visit Tobias last.

God has had his drink, Tobias thought.

That night, the ponds were silent.

In the fourth hour after the meridian the frogs began to fall.

The storm had calmed only a little after the short trip from the Bethlehem fields to Jerusalem. Its updrafts had retreated into the heavy clouds that darkened the sky over the palace and the neighborhoods nearby. Finally exhausted with their loads, the clouds released rains of which no one could recall the like into the sudden winds that foretold their arrival.

As the wind eased, the heavy rain began to rest upon the earth, delivering one, then two, then a thousand frogs, more, to the streets of Jerusalem.

The frogs were small and not long hatched. Some were still dragging what remained of their tadpole tails. But despite the rough eviction from their birthplace, most were none the worse for having been sucked into the sky and poured into the capital near the palace.

They hopped in every direction, searching for muddy puddles that felt like home. They gathered in courtyards. They climbed walls. They entered houses and shops through any crack they could find. Delighted children ignored their mothers and ran out into the rain to chase the misshapen alien creatures which, for all their strangeness, were comically athletic.

The citizens were startled at first. But soon they saw the frogs through the children's eyes and judged the infestation harmless, perhaps even an amusement offered by God to take people's minds off Judea's unsettled state and the ferment at the palace just a street or two over.

One small Frog climbed onto the sill of a shuttered window of the one person in the city who did not share the people's amusement.

❦

Herod was being dressed for the evening meal – he wondered what crowd of obsequious supplicants his ministers had rounded up for that night's repast – when the storm reached Jerusalem. His valet had come from a tour of the palace's windows, where he had marveled at the funny little bouncing green visitors. He laughed as he reported on the sight. But Herod was not entertained by the frogs' dance through the Jerusalem streets, and the valet snapped into a mood to match his master's.

"Perhaps your small crown tonight, my king? Or that lovely dried wreath from your last trip to –"

"Summon the Chief Priest."

"He's not in the city, my king," the valet said. "I heard he's gone to –"

"I don't care if he's on the beach at Gaza getting his beard oiled by one of his concubines he doesn't think I know about. Have a minister send for him before the sun sets."

Herod heard the shouts of the children over the wind and rain.

His body wanted to sigh but it hurt too much to take a deep breath.

I have governed with a strong arm for Rome, and this is my reward?

The simmering unrest in the countryside was threatening to spread to the capital. The wealthy, the damned rich, complaining about taxes. Bands of brigands robbing travelers and even his own tax collectors. Rome's support growing uncertain, and now they want to *count* everyone, they want to *list* everyone? Was Caesar, his old friend Augustus, questioning his collection of tribute to the Empire?

His own sons and even his *sister* – what mighty king ever had to deal with a *sister*? – circling the throne and scheming to squeeze their own asses into it when he died.

The pain in his gut and the cry from his spine and the ceaseless burning wet itch between his legs.

Now this, a storm in memory unseen bringing with it an army of creatures unsuited to any city, much less to the capital, much less to the palace, his palace.

From the skies, a visitation from heaven itself.

It had to mean something.

He nudged open the shutter a crack and peered out with one eye.

The eye went to the little Frog on the sill.

That cursed beast is smiling at me.

The Frog croaked.

Herod slammed the shutter and raged from the room. He would find a minister to arrange to move his throne from Jerusalem for a while. Caesarea Maritima would do. A pretty little palace on the coast of the Great Sea in Samaria, one of his favorites. He would rule from there for a season, perhaps two, let the tide support his bones and cool his flesh.

But not before he confirmed a thing or two with that randy High Priest he'd appointed.

Over the next couple of days, the frogs scattered and vanished.

CHAPTER 1

The World Stirs

THE BIG MAN on the big donkey considered himself a master of circumstances. Partly because he was a big man in a small world; partly because circumstances seemed always to match his desires and expectations, requiring little mastery to begin with. While he never knew what the days would bring, his history of success in life suggested to him that matters were always likely to conclude to his advantage.

He had many of the same big questions about life and death and everything that most people have when adolescence is finally shocked into adulthood, and those questions vexed him greatly at close of day when his mind was free to ask them. But from sunrise to sunset, he cheerfully faced whatever circumstances the day presented, as it was his understanding that those circumstances, however unknowable, would appear to him within a range of familiar reality.

His understanding will not survive this story.

❧

"Well, mighty Zac, what destiny do you suppose awaits me tomorrow at the house of Nathan?"

Zac rotated his ears toward the big man on his back, but as he recognized neither the sound nor the cadence of command, he continued his steady pace to Jericho.

The rhythm of Zac's pace was relaxing, almost hypnotic. The big man allowed himself to imagine the morrow as there was nowhere other than forward for Zac to go.

"Consider, Zac: I'm a man of size. My voice is loud. Every day I wrestle with stones and mortar and yet I find myself thinking that if I encounter the slightest resistance in Jerusalem tomorrow, you and I will start back for Nazareth before the sun sets."

The words meant nothing to Zac.

"I pray that God will quicken my mind and my tongue to deal with what I'll find there. I've grown to fear little in my life, but today I feel like a gladiator Caesar sends into the arena, not knowing if a sword will be in his hand or his belly."

Zac thought that a taste of water would be a good thing to happen to him.

"And let me add that I'm delighted to have your support on this journey."

Zac formed a vision of a neat pile of barley straw.

The big man laughed. "Zac, my faithful friend, you're the most magnificent donkey in Galilee, but your conversational skills could use a spot of polish."

Zac's hooves on the hardpack were the only disturbance to the stone stillness of the desert road.

"Ah, you're wise to save your breath. We'll rest, first shade we spot."

Sandar the Builder stiffened. A gentle unseen finger touched his spine and brought his senses to attention.

Zac felt Sandar's shock and stopped.

The sky was alive.

It was clear, and a pure even blue stretched over the desert road from horizon to horizon. Sandar could feel rather than see a heartbeat in the unchanging azure above him. There was something warm and growing beyond the firmament, or within it.

A storm ready to boil up out of nothing, perhaps. They were not rare in these hills as winter surrendered to spring, but Sandar knew that what he felt was not a mere change in the weather.

The sky changed. Sandar's alert sharpened. The dome began to admit lighter and darker shades – still blue, still clear, but now folding and unfolding into vague shapes flowing through it, swirling in and around each other, moving to form themselves into something recognizable. But only for an eyeblink: One moment the shapes were, the next moment were not, a hazy crowd of floating beings made out of sky.

And there was something new emerging beneath the firmament, on this very roadside.

At the edge of his vision he sensed a sparkle in a rock on the side of the road. He turned his head quickly to see it, but it was gone. Two more sparkles on the other side of the road. Sandar spun to see them; gone.

In the dry hills, the sandgrey stones themselves became unusually vivid to his eye, with shades and hues he had never before seen. Their layered colors, some of them, vibrated. Now there were many sparkles in the rocks, too many to hide from him, and they ignited his eyes.

The branches of the roadside bushes and trees, usually sagging and brittle as they waited for rain, seemed to rise in expectation.

Or supplication?

Or praise?

Flowers he had never before noticed in the desert bloomed in the brush. Or did they? He could smell them, he thought, but he could not . . . .

Zac skittered sideways as a dule of doves, or something living, rose from the roadside and spiraled into the sky and disappeared. Were they agitated, or excited with some invisible delight?

He perceived he was an audience of one, and listened for the whisper of what the scene was working to say. He felt something was calling on him to observe this slice of the world with a piercing clarity, if he would. He looked at the landscape and sky with the intent to see them truly, to satisfy himself that what he was seeing was real, as he understood what was real.

But just as the color and sound and movement had filled his senses to their rim, everything stopped like a dream on waking.

Nothing before him but the desert's drab and airless stillness. Just rocks and a few scrub plants and a bird or two, and silence. Olive trees motionless as if carved from stone. Nothing to see but the desert hills east of Jericho, as brown and scrubby and unwelcoming as they had ever been on any of his journeys over and through them. Yet, also like a dream on waking, a dream that lingers after the eyes have found the familiar shapes of the bedchamber, the sensation of something waiting to come alive remained, pricked his skin; the scene around and above him just at the margin of his awareness seemed possessed of some secret vital essence that sparked and hummed.

What was causing this lively, playful, now-you-see-it-and-don't dance of the light?

It felt almost joyful.

"Did you –"

Sandar shook his head. "Talking to a donkey." He nudged Zac to get going.

Perhaps, he thought, there was something different about this day, or something changed in his life, or the world. Perhaps he was seeing the plain surfaces around him clearly and truly for the first time. But why today? Why him? Why on this particular path of the many he traveled in his life?

And, he thought, there was this:

The next day would decide on his life going one way rather than another. Maybe the thought of his upcoming appointment in Jerusalem had prodded his mind to attention and freshly opened his consciousness to drama in the land and sky that had really always been there. Perhaps the anticipation of what he might encounter in the city awakened some seldom-used sense that shuddered and yawned as it rose to focus for the first time.

Sandar had made this journey from Nazareth many times in his business – south through the Jordan Valley, an overnight stop in Jericho, then west over the desert hills to the capital. This visit was in his personal interest. Since he left Nazareth he thought about things he wanted to say at the house of Nathan, and things he wanted to hear. He shut his eyes against the shimmering roadside and rehearsed his words, and his responses to what he might hear in return.

But focus as he might on what lay ahead for him, the oddness of the day kept intruding. The spectacle of the desert come alive had ended, but Sandar could not shake the feeling that the landscape still lived, perhaps now only napping, waiting to perform for him once again. As Zac bore him towards Jericho, Sandar remained distracted by the memory of the foreign glitter of the road and the stones and the scrub, and whatever had been moving in the shapeless sky. They were the same road and rocks and bushes he'd passed a dozen times before, but today they seemed ready to burst with a message that only they could deliver, but that they held back at the hand of another.

As he and Zac ascended into the hills of Judea, he came to feel an odd comfort in the foreignness of the day. He grew content to let his imagination assemble the world as it would. He needed to be relaxed for Jerusalem.

Zac startled and squealed. Sandar nearly fell off the big donkey as he spun to face north.

"Ho ho ho Zac!" Sandar said. "Hold up, now. What is it?"

On a boulder atop a nearby rise, Sandar saw the Lion in silhouette against the bright sky.

It sat facing the man and the donkey. Sandar wondered how long it had been there, and if it was hungry.

When Zac saw the Lion that he had only smelled before, he calmed.

There were many lions to be found in the Torah and the other holy books. In this dry age, though, they were seldom seen. It was unusual to see them in the desert, and even shepherds' reports were few.

The Lion was still. Sandar wondered if some prankster had propped a lion silhouette up there to frighten travelers. Until the silhouette shook its mane, looked to one side, and licked its nose. Sandar made sure his *gladius* was within easy reach.

"I'll remember this trip," Sandar told Zac. "But these visions are not getting us closer to Jericho, where we'll both need a drink, in my case something more potent than what I have in my bag."

When he looked back to the boulder, the Lion was gone.

Perhaps, Sandar thought, he should find some shade and have a sip of that water, get some bread in his stomach. Close his eyes and rest for a bit. Offer Zac a sloppy slurp or two from the goatskin. The desert miracle had not detained him long; he was making time satisfactory to his schedule. Even though Zac was doing all the work, a stop to rest his eyes might calm his vision. He would look about and see the near-dead landscape for what it was.

But the sky, the stones, the light, that Lion, the thrumming pulse of this day . . . something, something.

It was like the world was holding its breath.

CHAPTER 2

Sandar the Builder

SANDAR THE BUILDER was the largest man in Nazareth – some said the largest in Galilee, perhaps even Judea – unusually tall and broad even for a Gentile, and powerful up and down his frame. When he was a boy in his small village north and east of Nazareth the children would tease him, calling him the "Goliath" who would fall before David's sling. But his kindly nature and his acts to protect smaller children and aid them with his strength transformed it into a nickname of affection. As he grew into a tall and athletic adolescence, the children no longer used it. He entered into a rangy, muscular manhood, and became known as one who did not unfairly press his size in his dealings, but was instead generous with his strength.

His donkey Zac mirrored his owner's size and strength, and even seemed to reflect Sandar's soft temper and reliability. An average donkey of Galilee would have struggled under a man of Sandar's size. While Sandar could walk for many miles unaided, a man of his position was expected to have a sound and handsome donkey. And, while he was still some years from middle age, Sandar was no longer a boy; the journeys his business required with the tools he needed were now best undertaken with the stoic and steady Zac beneath him.

Sandar did not remember the parents one or another god had given him. He learned from elders at the synagogue that his mother was Greek and his father Roman, although it was said both exhibited a fair strain from one or more Northmen who had entered their lines by means honorable or dubious. As he grew, he could see them all in the looking-glass. They had abandoned him as a small child as they fled Galilee for reasons he was unable to discover. The elders were evasive about whether his mother and father had been married.

He was raised in a Jewish family and learned its language and its faith; his acceptance as a Jew by conversion, while aided by his temperament and skills, and not a little by his size and beauty, was always more formal than felt. But Sandar ignored the small discomforts of his ancestry, and as the years went by those who knew him did the same. He knew the warmth of his welcome in Nathan's home would be sincere.

In fact, his aptitude and appetite for learning brought him attention as a star student at the synagogue. He was quick of mind; speech came easily to him – perhaps, sometimes, a little too easily as he was impatient to interrupt his elders. He thought about becoming a priest himself, but despite his welcome into the community, his teachers discouraged pursuit of a position where devotion was at least partly measured by one's bloodline.

His priestly turn of mind had given him a taste for things that were eternal and certain; he began his adult life as a worker in stone and brick. He added carpentry to his offerings. As his skill grew, he began making fine furniture for wealthier Nazarenes. He soon added the construction of homes and workplaces and sheds to his services throughout Galilee, beyond Nazareth to the surrounding towns and villages, north to Cana and Capernaum and even Tyre, and south to Jericho and Hebron in Judea. His structures were recognized for their robustness and formal elegance. With the quality of his work and the honesty of his dealings, his fame and wealth grew. When commissions were completed he would personally craft a small sculpture as a gift to his client, or perhaps an exquisite tiny barrow or masks or carved animals or balls for the children. Over the years the circumstances of his work brought him into contact with the powerful and wealthy of the several districts of Israel. He could get by in Latin and Greek when necessary to his business.

It was a good life.

But something was wrong.

It needed to change.

Jerusalem tomorrow.

⋘

After the Lion vanished, Zac maintained his usual indifference to his owner's attempts at conversation and kept walking. Sandar realized he'd been talking to stones; a soft laugh rumbled up from his belly. Despite his prediction to Zac, he knew he would not be turning back unless he got an unconditional rejection in Jerusalem he was frankly not expecting. The conduct of his business had persuaded him that anything, anything, can be negotiated no matter the distance between adversaries or the strength of their convictions. And the bright stones along his path – the roadside rubble fairly vibrated with some inscrutable intention – perhaps they would advise him on his mission the next day in Jerusalem as they glittered under the naked sun.

The route from Nazareth to Jerusalem through Samaria might have been a little shorter, a little faster, but this time he decided on the flatter and greener route through the Jordan Valley. The Samaritans could be difficult with Jewish travelers, although Sandar's size and color meant that he was usually either ignored or assisted with peaceable passage. His journey down the Valley would take him as far south as Jericho; then, if it did not rain, it was only one long day west over the desert hills of Judea into Jerusalem.

He was glad to be away from Nazareth and the projects that awaited his attention there. As his third decade approached its end, he needed to think clearly about his life. Lately he had been out of sorts; friends and colleagues had noticed it. The week before he had moved to whip a workman who had displeased him. But he caught himself and apologized to the man and sent him home with a piece of silver. He had barely ever raised his voice to a workman before, and never his hand. Something was changing in him.

He had gone to the synagogue to pray and ask

forgiveness. He said the words and left money with the priest, but when he left the old building he felt no better than when he had walked in. In the synagogue he had paid more attention to the disrepair of the place and what he might do to strengthen it than to the state of his soul. Perhaps he would donate his talents to this congregation which, he had to admit, as a single man he did not know as well as he might.

Sandar was grateful for the traditions and laws of his parents' faith and he did his best to honor them. But as the years had come and gone, and he was no longer pre-occupied with mere survival and advancement, he found himself thinking more and more about – he did not have a word for it. The word he could feel forming in his head was *Why?*

The question seemed trivial and profound at the same time. He knew the Greek gods, and the Roman gods, too, and, of course, the God of the Jewish household where he was raised. He was content enough to believe in gods as circumstances demanded, but the single formless God of the Jews appealed to his love of order and his sense of what an ultimate being should be. And that God had a written history, too; not just the myths of Homer or the oral reports, but of men and women who knew of this God – knew Him, heard His voice, even spoke back to Him (sometimes rather impudently, Sandar noted), from their time living their lives on the earth. Some of them had even interacted with Him, told in stories Sandar found more believable than the accounts of the battling and fornicating and lying gods of the myths of the invaders from the west. The old ones wrote down what they knew of this God; the priests taught it at synagogue.

But Greek, Roman, or Hebrew, he saw no signs of the gods' authority or power, no signs of their goodness. No evidence of the eyes to believe in one rather than another. Nothing, beyond the odd ancient Hebrew laws and sometimes dubious histories, even to *believe* at all. How should he know whether a life should even *have* meaning – should be *something* – beyond adherence to those old laws, and the new ones the Romans and the provincial governors had invented? Even the God of the Jews seemed to have fallen silent hundreds of years ago, if the texts were to be believed. He believed them.

He did not speak of his thoughts to others. He recognized them as strange, even dangerous. Sandar was a working man but he had become a man of wealth, at greater leisure than most, and he had the luxury of time to think such thoughts, and the sense to keep them thoughts.

And when he thought about the world, and the laws, and his life of waking and working and sleeping and waking to the same again, and he saw the life of the city around him, and in the small towns he visited, and in the stories of the pictures of men and animals the stars made and of which Homer sang and of the invisible gods and the invisible God of his parents, a conviction came gradually upon him.

It was a conviction upon which he hoped to act successfully tomorrow in Jerusalem.

CHAPTER 3

The Searchers

SANDAR TOLD THE hostler at the stable in Jericho that he would be leaving before sunrise the next day. He settled with him for Zac's feed and board.

The three sleek Arabian stallions in the stalls were big, much bigger than the horses of Israel, of which there were few outside of Rome's cavalry. God's ancient prohibition on acquiring horses had gradually faded in memory, but despite their speed and strength they were costly and expensive to maintain and only a few wealthy citizens owned them. But here were some beauties. Sumptuously embroidered blankets and other tack were draped over the stable walls of each of them.

Sandar walked out of the stable into the cool night. He was ready to get to his room and go to sleep after today's dancing desert and sky had siphoned so much of his attention, but now there was something he needed to do.

He headed toward the light and noise of a large tavern nearby.

Down the street, a commotion. In the dark, Sandar could barely discern three people in a doorway. Two men on the ground, surrounded by a few sacks. A tall man with a tall hat stood over them, speaking angrily and threatening them with his staff. He could not hear what the tall angry man was saying. One of the men on the ground was responding calmly, but was drowned out by the tall man's threats. The pair had stopped in their travels to rest, Sandar surmised; perhaps to sleep, too poor to lodge at the inn. And now, perhaps, harmlessly trespassing.

Wait – no. Was it? – it was, a man and woman on the ground.

The tall man raised his staff. Sandar began to run toward them.

The man on the ground stood up and raised his hands. The tall man relaxed his staff and stopped yelling, took a step back. Sandar stopped.

The woman – yes, certainly a woman, short, heavy, her head covered – stood with difficulty. She and the man gathered their bags. The tall man resumed his scolding as the couple left the doorway.

Sandar watched as the man and woman disappeared away from him into the dark.

᠁

Jericho was seldom a destination, Sandar thought. It was a place to travel through. The men in the tavern all lived elsewhere, away from the eyes of their families or places where their behavior might be reported.

He stood in its doorway, where his rare size and light golden hair quieted the crowd briefly before it returned to its various interests. A woman who might have been judged lovely had she left her face unpainted approached and whispered in his ear. He shook his head and brushed her away. Three dice games; an old man with his head on a table in a puddle of drool; two men rising to fight in a far corner.

He saw the three men he was looking for and moved toward their table. Each was wearing a robe rich with color and illuminated with gold and silver threads, the tight weaves shining even in the dull light of the tavern. Each wore a turban with jewels embedded in the style of its wearer's homeland.

"The evening's greetings to you, gentlemen," Sandar said.

"And to you as well, sir." Of the three, the man who spoke, named Melchior, looked most at home in the tavern. He had a light scar down his left cheek and a fierce cast to his eyes, and the bulky robe could not hide his muscular build. His beard was kinked and unoiled. He looked toward the brewing fight in the corner as if considering joining it.

"Are you the owners of the three fine Arabians I saw in the stable?"

"We are," Melchior said.

"They are splendid," Sandar said, "and beautifully appointed. I've thought of acquiring a horse."

The youngest of the three men was Balthazar, a black African, slightly built with a graceful manner and a face with the symmetry of a sunflower. Sandar noticed that he seemed uneasy in the tavern, looking about the place as Sandar approached, but now glad to have a new listener who was friendly and large. "There was a regal donkey of some size tethered outside the inn," Balthazar said. "Would that be yours?"

"It would indeed, young man," Sandar said. "And, if I'm truthful with myself, Zac is satisfactory for my purposes."

"I'm thinking I might prefer a donkey to my horse," the third man said. He was old and fat and wore the biggest turban and his name was Old Caspar. His hair was grey and neither it nor his beard had been trimmed in his memory. His beard and robe featured crumbs from the light repast still on the table. "I'm more accustomed to a donkey, and they are smarter, and they will fight a wolf. Better for the desert, better for the hills. Shorter, too, easier for these fat old bones to mount."

Melchior noted the big man's good robe and sandals and groomed appearance. Few men went beardless these days. "You have something more than livestock on your mind."

"I do. When I saw the horses I thought to tell their riders that I've met travelers from Jerusalem who warn of robbers on the way, if you're going that way."

Melchior said, "We're grateful for your report. Our mission has quite enough hindrances already. For that news, join us." Melchior had already found an empty cup and poured some wine.

"Ah," Sandar said, "thank you for your courtesy, but I'm unusually weary from an unusual day on the Nazareth road."

"Unusual weariness and unusual days call for the usual medicine," Old Caspar said. "Sit with us, sir."

Sandar sat and took a long swallow, his first in several hours. He wasn't sure if the strong wine cleared his head, or filled it.

"We don't take your news lightly," Melchior said, "but we travel with men of Herod's guard and their servants, some strong young men to handle the camels and donkeys with supplies and tents for our trip." He waved his arm at some men at nearby tables with a rough military look to them.

"Herod!" Sandar thought this explained why these opulent travelers still had these hats on their heads, or their heads at all.

"We have his commission to search for . . . something that interests him," Melchior said.

"For your sakes, I hope you find it!"

"Aye, we'll find *something*, I assure you," Old Caspar said. The three men laughed uneasily.

"Forgive me," Sandar said, "but you don't look like men Herod would send to search for something in the desert. I'm well acquainted with Galilee and Judea, and some with Samaria. If you can tell me what you seek, perhaps I can assist you."

Melchior glanced at Old Caspar, who gave him a tiny nod.

"We're seeking a person, perhaps . . . destined to perform some special task."

Sandar looked at each of the three men in turn.

"You're readers of the stars," he said.

"Did the stars on our robes give us away?" Old Caspar said.

Melchior chewed his bread. "You remember the rains around the turn of the year."

Sandar laughed. "Remember? I expected to see Noah sailing by!"

"The storms were especially severe south of Jerusalem. Funnel clouds, clouds of legend, almost never seen! They reached into some ponds and marshes and collected thousands of newly-hatched frogs which the winds kept aloft until the front reached Jerusalem. And then –"

"A storm of frogs," Sandar said.

"Countless small frogs all over the city, but especially in the neighborhoods around the palace."

"The children were thrilled," Old Caspar said, "and cooks learned a new delicacy."

"But Herod," Melchior said, "he was not thrilled."

"Perhaps he was remembering the plague of frogs God brought upon Egypt," Sandar said.

"Perhaps he was," Melchior said, "but what is certain is that he thought it was a sign of *some* kind, and not one good for his throne. He left the capital and moved the government to the palace at Caesarea, where, I believe, he continues to sit. If he is able." Old Caspar snickered.

Sandar said, "But you – you're not from Israel."

"Very astute," Balthazar said.

Melchior continued. "Herod was dissatisfied with interpretations he received from the palace astrologers. He solicited readings from courts of the Empire and beyond."

"When we're not parsing the stars, we consult amphibians," Old Caspar said.

"And you three – your visions matched."

Melchior nodded. "They did. And now we're hoping to find the reality behind those visions."

"The frogs," Sandar said. "You say they were newly born and appeared to invade the capital. So you seek . . . a child? Who might . . . somehow threaten Israel?"

Melchior peered at Sandar with great interest. "Perhaps we should get you one of these hats. We took it as a sign foretelling the appearance of one – perhaps a child – who will lead the Jews."

"Your readings fed his unease." Sandar felt a little uneasy himself at this coincidence. "Your art is a mystery. Astonishing that frogs suggested the same reading to each –"

"Do you know the prophecies?" Balthazar interjected.

Melchior placed his hand on Balthazar's arm. Old Caspar coughed ostentatiously.

"Herod invited each of us to Caesarea." Melchior looked at his colleagues. "We all went." Sandar detected a slight note of regret.

Balthazar said, "He actually *seemed* pleased when we presented our reading. He favored us with a commission, and this guard. Even gold as a gift for this . . . person."

"I travel Galilee and Judea, sometimes Samaria, but I must say that I haven't heard news of any young person with unusual skills or gifts beyond his age. You seek a boy?"

"The prophecies speak of –" Balthazar said, but Melchior cut him off again.

"Quite likely a boy," Melchior said. "But as the person we seek is unknown, and may be extraordinary in respects that have not yet been revealed to us, perhaps a girl."

"You have a most unusual and difficult commission from Herod."

Old Caspar said, "Yes, and that's why our search requires three of us."

Sandar threw his head back and laughed a deep, hearty laugh. "Indeed, three times the usual magical wisdom would seem to be called for!"

"Your interest in our work is gratifying to hear," Melchior said. "Not everyone believes the skies have stories to guide us here on earth. But Herod – for all that some might say against him, he's learned and remains curious even from his throne."

"How do you hope to search for a single small person in our vast and varied lands?" Sandar said. "Surely the stars do not speak with such precision, and it doesn't sound like the little frogs provided much direction."

"We speak to the leaders of the synagogues and persons of influence who know the towns we visit," Balthazar said. "And we're hoping for more signs that will allow us to refine our inquiries, and perhaps even to be drawn to this special person."

"I hope your search is fruitful," Sandar said. "I say to you, gentlemen: If your searches take you to Nazareth, please do me the honor of asking after Sandar the Builder. My name is known in Galilee. I can stable your animals, even the camels, and ensure proper quarters for your men. And I can promise appropriate lodging for men of your station."

"We began our search north from Caesarea," Melchior said. "The Samaritans were, shall we say, unhelpful. We did visit Nazareth, although briefly."

"I'm surprised I hadn't heard of your visit," Sandar said.

"The chief priest of the synagogue there discouraged our inquiries and rather colorfully urged us to move on without canvassing the citizens," Old Caspar said.

"Ah, yes," Sandar said, "old Baruch, he would not be one to credit frogs. Perhaps if you return I can open some doors."

"We're headed west tomorrow," Melchior said, "but should we return north to Nazareth we will ask after Sandar without fail."

Sandar said, "I'm honored to be in the presence of magi. Perhaps I'll engage you to cast my own future as the fixed stars and wandering planets might disclose. I've lately found my sleep disturbed with . . . questions."

"What questions?" Balthazar said.

"If you visit Nazareth, perhaps. It wasn't my purpose to occupy you with my concerns."

"Ah," Old Caspar said, "but we're gratified that you respect our gifts. The people of Israel seem to have lost their faith that the heavens have wisdom to guide us here on earth. We'd be honored to hear the questions a man of commerce asks when the sun sets."

Sandar took another sip of wine. He smiled and shook his head.

"We're friends sharing a cup, eh?" Melchior said.

"Aye," Sandar said, "and these strong Jericho cups threaten to soften my guard."

"Look here," Old Caspar said, "there's more," and freshened Sandar's cup. Sandar stared at his cup and he began to speak.

"I build the homes and halls of Nazareth and beyond. God has favored me with strength and skill and sense, and the silver and gold have followed."

Melchior said, "There would seem to be little to question in that!"

"You magicians look to the skies and divine the meaning of what you see there." The wine loosened his voice. "But I look at my feet from an elevation greater than any man's in Galilee, and think: Why must I stand on the ground at all? On this ground? What holds me here when the sky is great above me and filled with the sun and moon and stars and the rain that gives life? Why are the great world and sky forbidden to me? Why am I rooted to the hard soil of Israel like an ancient cedar? Will I leave behind nothing but buildings that will crumble and rot?"

The magi shifted in their seats.

"God forgive me these questions."

Balthazar said, "I'm certain God hears your questions."

"And he'll answer him in His time," Old Caspar said.

"Aye," Sandar said, "and I fear those answers. Today on the road from Nazareth . . . I was alone . . . the earth and the sky . . . it was like the earth had a secret it could not wait to tell."

"My friends and I seek signs of just such boldness," Balthazar said. "Perhaps one will grace our road tomorrow."

Sandar said, "The road tomorrow." He emptied his cup, and pushed back from the table. "I have business in

Jerusalem; Zac and I will rise with the rooster. I bid you good night with thanks for your unexpected company. Remember Sandar in Nazareth, my home is yours. God rest you, gentlemen, and speed your search."

Sandar nodded to the magi and turned to leave. He thought of something and turned back to the three men.

"I never learned your names."

Old Caspar said, "Nobody ever remembers our names."

CHAPTER 4

At Rest

THE MAN LOOKED up at the moon. "It will be full tomorrow."

"A blessing," the woman said. "Or, perhaps not. We can be seen as well as see."

"We should rest," the man said. "You should rest."

"No one here to throw us out of the desert."

"That shopkeeper," the man said. "The day may come he'll regret becoming part of our journey in that way."

"Perhaps God wanted us to keep moving. The man was a tool for His purpose."

"God doesn't want you to faint on the road."

"It's so," the woman said. "My dreams neglected to warn of practical hardships."

The man spotted a small clearing away from the road. He guided the woman there and they spread a blanket in some moonshade and lay down.

"We shouldn't sleep long," the woman said.

"The birds and sky will wake us long before sunup."

The man lay on his back and looked up at the Pole Star.

"If my friends are right about distances," the man said, "from here, Bethlehem tomorrow night."

The woman was still trying to get comfortable. The baby was bucking like an unbroken ass. "*If* they're right?"

The man and the woman laughed softly.

"That's good," the woman said, "good we can laugh," and she closed her eyes and was asleep.

CHAPTER 5

The Guard and the Magi

BEFORE HE LEFT the tavern, Sandar paused at one of the tables where the military men were sitting. They were drinking and laughing but Sandar's large shadow caught their attention.

Sandar said, "Have I the honor of addressing the guard of Herod the King?"

One of the men, more colorfully attired than the others, leaned back in his seat to take in the sight of the big man before him. "You have that honor," he said. "And who is addressing the guard?"

"I'm Sandar of Nazareth."

"What was your business with the star men, Sandar the Nazarene?" the guard asked. He finished his cup of wine and raised it for more. An innkeeper rushed to fill it.

"No business. I'd admired their fine horses and, taking them for travelers, wanted to alert them to reports of robbers on these roads. I so advise you as well."

"Would you be one of them?" the guard said. "You look to be a man not unacquainted with putting the sword to the use for which it's intended."

Sandar said, "It would be a foolish robber indeed who made his face known to those who guard Herod. I'm a man of business traveling early tomorrow to Jerusalem."

"Your warning is well taken," the guard said. "I'm Ogen, chief of this squad. There are twelve of us under arms, although we have laid aside our armor for this evening's leisure. Also attendants, some of whom are old enough to wield a sword." He gestured to a table with younger men. "It's doubtful robbers would take us on."

"Aye," Sandar said, "but the greater the guard, the greater the treasure. Robbers' minds are enflamed with the reward, and not the risk. And with tax collections making their way to Jerusalem, a bandit of vision might assemble a more formidable team to greet a party of such obvious means."

"And certain companions obviously not accustomed to violence." Ogen inclined his head toward the astrologers' table.

"A fair point," Sandar said. "Although they made it to our land from beyond the Empire."

"Their good fortune in that regard, and Herod's command, are the only thing keeping me watching their flanks," Ogen said. "That they arrived at Caesarea in one piece wearing all that finery does intrigue me that their mission may be blessed by one god or another."

"What is Herod's interest?"

Sandar judged the small smile that appeared on Ogen's face something other than amusement.

Ogen said, "Herod does not share his motivations with his humble soldiers."

"The object of the magi's search must be a special child indeed," Sandar said.

"Yes, but if he even exists, only a child. Foretold by frogs, pish."

"You doubt?"

"Whether he exists or is only a fraud invented by the star men to pry a commission out of Herod is of no interest to me. I'm a soldier, born to the sword and the battlefield, but my orders are to protect Herod and do his work. I shall do both, whether in the palace or the wilderness. He ordered me to protect the star men" – he took another generous swallow – "so I do. Pausing for a cup when I'm able."

There was little about Herod that did not trouble Sandar, and the obscurity of Ogen's meaning was ominous. What sense in suggesting that Herod required protection from a child?

"Indeed," he said, "robbers who don't think twice about attacking your party will be in for a bloody lesson."

"You have spoken truly, Nazarene."

"Godspeed, then, to you and your men," Sandar said. He bowed slightly to Ogen and turned to leave the tavern.

Ogen raised his cup in the direction of the departing Sandar. "Herod's health."

⤎

"'Perhaps a girl,' Melchior?" Old Caspar lifted an eyebrow and smiled.

Melchior shrugged. "Our searches have not been so fruitful that we should narrow our reading of what the frogs might have been suggesting." He turned to Balthazar. "And I didn't want to be too specific with our new friend. Not everyone finds the prophecies credible after all this time."

"Wise," Balthazar said.

The men had been searching for weeks with no encouraging interviews and no signs.

Balthazar was usually the one who nudged the others to voice their intentions for the days ahead. "He or she, young or grown, what is our plan?"

Melchior tapped the table. "We will search. There will be a sign. My instinct tells me Judea is the place. Jerusalem has many souls and many children and many places for children to hide themselves."

"Micah the prophet says Israel's ruler will rise from Bethlehem," Balthazar said. "From David's tree, out of Jesse's line."

"And we'll visit there, should Jerusalem disappoint," Melchior said. "But did Micah know the stars? Did Isaiah mention a sign? No. We're advanced in knowledge from the old ones' time, we know more of the stars and the bright wanderers among them. And the frogs – they were visitors from the skies, if not from the heavenly sphere itself."

Balthazar looked nervously around the room.

"There is something tugging at the heart of our young colleague from Aegyptus," Old Caspar said.

"I sometimes wonder if we were – if I was – right to

respond to Herod's summons and petition for a commission," Balthazar said.

Melchior was startled, having wondered this himself, but said, "You question that our readings were correct?"

"Oh, that I do not doubt."

"Then what is your meaning?"

"I sometimes feel as if we were flattered at his invitation and rose to his bait by promoting this search."

Old Caspar said, "I've been telling myself that my desire to receive this commission didn't overcome my good sense."

"So you've had questions, too?" Melchior said.

"Yes, if I'm an honest man of the stars, which I tell myself I am. I fail to picture Herod on his knees before anyone but Caesar."

Melchior drained his cup and considered his response. He had thought through the same question and imagined an answer satisfactory to himself.

"Keep your voices low," Melchior said. "Herod is not our king, but he is *a* king. He has the friendship of Augustus and is respected by our own kings. Even Quirinius secured our safe passage through Syria, yours and mine, Caspar."

"I know my concerns are tardy," Balthazar said. "But in my bed I ask if I should have considered with greater care whether Herod's interest in a new Hebrew king is genuine."

Melchior leaned into the table and lowered his voice. "The Jews are a quiet people, but they are restless, oppressed by both Rome and Herod. They resent the taxes on them, the tribute to Rome on top of Herod's. News of revolts in the countryside are inspiring the poor in the cities to resist his reign. He is old and in poor health, we saw that. And his throne is bedeviled by unrest within the palace. His sons – those he has not executed – are said to quarrel over succession even as his cock rots from the dripping disease!"

Melchior swirled the wine remaining in this cup and sat back. "Or so I've heard."

Old Caspar said, "With all respect due, Melchior, what do Herod's family problems and the state of his cock have to do with whether he is sincere in supporting our search?"

Melchior half-smiled, then half-asked: "Perhaps, with all his troubles, he seeks an ally sent of God."

"Perhaps," Old Caspar said.

Emboldened by his question having been taken seriously, Balthazar said, "Do you believe he wishes to visit and pay homage to the child, or whoever we find?"

"It is what he said," Melchior said.

"It is what he said," Old Caspar said.

"It's not for us to pass judgment on his honesty other than to judge him honest – being king, you know," Melchior said, but there was uncertainty in his tone.

He tilted his cup to see what was left in it. "My friends, reading stars and signs for the powerful and wealthy – this is what we *do*! Without their patronage, we're no more than street-scrambling fortune-tellers! This is no time to be questioning Herod's motives. He's given us *gold* for this child!"

"Ogen holds it," Old Caspar said, "but yes, he has."

Melchior's words poured out as the wine settled and his companions evaded his eye. "Let us consider ourselves, gentlemen. We are men judged to possess a certain kind of special knowledge, much prized among our peoples. That knowledge is sought by our own rulers and is respected in other lands; Herod trusted the letters of introduction Old Caspar and I presented from our own sovereigns.

"Is it too much to say that God has entrusted us with an understanding of the language of the skies and signs and portents? And being blessed in this way, do we not have a duty to provide the truths we read there to leaders of the people who have an interest in such things? Of course, I don't deny that this is our living – yes, we sought the commission and Herod has promised us much upon a successful search.

"But if we are not honest, and not faithful to our rulers, will kings and priests continue to seek our counsel? Is it our office to question their judgment in the uses to which it will be put?"

"That's my worry," Balthazar said. "I don't know what his judgment will be if our search is successful. And I fear his judgment if it isn't."

Melchior was growing irritated. "We have heard his words that he seeks the one so that he may honor him. He has given us gold to present to this child. He has given us a guard and donkeys and camels. We can *only* believe him. If we were not prepared to deal with him faithfully we were fools in seeking the commission."

Old Caspar and Balthazar shared small smiles. Both were eager to change the subject. "That's so," old Caspar said, "but whatever our view of Herod's motives, the stars have been mute since we began our search. I pray nightly for a toad to come whisper in my ear."

"Our visitor told us of a sign of the desert reborn," Balthazar said. "Say, did you not find the Builder quick of mind and gracious of speech?"

"I did, Balthazar," Melchior said. "And large."

"The Builder," Old Caspar mused. "There *was* something about him, was there not?"

"As we are speaking of signs," Balthazar said, "could he be the sign we seek? Something unusual, something in Judea, a man with mystery about him. In fact, with the authority he seems to possess, might he even be . . . and he's headed to Jerusalem for some 'business,' he said!"

"That thought crossed my mind," Old Caspar said, "as he did project a regal way, and a generous spirit. And he found us, who are seeking the king. But there was light in his eye and hair, and his profile – he was not Jewish. And at his age, were he to be a ruler, he would have declared himself and been exhorting the Jews. If he is a king, he betrayed little awareness of it."

"And remember his nighttime disquiet," Melchior said. "We seek one with answers, not questions."

"Anyone planning to displace Herod would need something more than a big donkey," Old Caspar said.

"He did say he was headed to Jerusalem," Melchior said. "Perhaps he can clear out the robbers."

"In some ways," Balthazar said, a little dreamily, "he and we are seeking the same thing."

Melchior returned to their search: "I feel we're seeking a child of early years, perhaps a baby. Even a child of three or four, if able to speak and a king of Israel, would surely have made himself known somehow, or appeared extraordinary in some way, and we should have heard of him from our inquiries."

"I agree," Balthazar said, "and so my concern we have

heard nothing and are looking for a babe who cannot make himself known to us, or to others who could direct us to him. Without a sign we – we will fail. And Ogen knows it. He's stirring up the servants and the camel hands, and he is making insinuations with the other soldiers."

"Herod should be glad we have given Ogen and his cohort something to do outside the palace," Melchior said. "These are times that try the loyalty even of seasoned men of arms. But we'll be traveling to Jerusalem tomorrow. The men and boys will visit their families, and some will seek out women who themselves seek to be found. Perhaps the grumbling will ease. We must keep searching."

Old Caspar said, "I'm thinking we may have been too hasty in rebuking our scholarly young colleague from the southlands with his suggestion of Bethlehem from the prophets. Quite aside from honoring the authority of Micah and Isaiah and the rest," he said, "I heard some bad news. I didn't want to say it with the Builder present."

"What news?" Melchior said.

"I heard that Herod has returned his throne to Jerusalem."

The men were quiet.

"Ogen's bored of our search and has scorned it from the beginning," Old Caspar said. "He wants to haul us back before Herod. If we stop in Jerusalem now, we might never leave."

Melchior said, "I would not like to report to him that our search so far hasn't found the foretold king of the Jews that the frogs portended."

"Not just *the* foretold," Old Caspar said. *"Our* foretold."

"An even greater threat to our necks," Melchior said. He unconsciously stroked his beard.

Balthazar said, "Might he be relieved that we've found no future king?"

"No," Melchior said.

"I fear we were persuasive before him, and united in our persuasiveness," Old Caspar said.

"I've made inquiries," Balthazar said. "There's a route to Bethlehem that branches south before Jerusalem."

"Bethlehem must be small, I'm thinking, few little ones," Old Caspar said. "Our search may go quickly."

"Ogen will not be pleased," Melchior said. "He's been looking forward to Jerusalem's easy women and easier ale."

"The guard never leaves the palace," Balthazar said. "They won't notice we've steered them down the road to Bethlehem."

"And when they do," Old Caspar said, "better to face Ogen's wrath than Herod's."

"The odds still favor Jerusalem," Melchior said, "but I travel with men of sense, for which I'm grateful. It's two of three for Bethlehem." He raised his cup. "A final taste before we follow the trail of the prophets," he said. "And may God keep the Builder safe and his blades sharp."

"And may a sign become known to us," Balthazar said.

❧

Ogen swayed in the doorway of his bedchamber. He carried his wine cup from the tavern. He put it down and shrugged off his cloak with difficulty. Shuffling over to the stacked blankets, he tried to lower himself gently, but he lost his balance and pitched onto them, with just enough waking awareness to roll onto his back before he passed out.

The Spirits drifted into the bedchamber through the window and the door and the ceiling and the walls. They filled the room, seen but unseen, swirling in and around each other like milk stirred into soup. There were three, there were twenty, there were forty, there were four. Neither male nor female, and both, a soft and comforting harmony accompanied their dance. When a face appeared among them, it was smiling; the Spirits were happy.

Two stroked the face of the sleeping Ogen. He grinned and woke. The two ghostly Spirits, now women, were beautiful to his eyes.

One of the Spirits reached into his chest and pulled out his glistening heart and showed it to him and laughed. It was beating, black.

Ogen screamed and grabbed for his heart, but the Spirit held it beyond his reach. All the Spirits were laughing now.

A large Heron appeared at the open window. It lifted its great grey wings and dove into the room. It flapped around the bedchamber, trying to herd the Spirits with its wings and drive them out. The Spirits continued to laugh as they teased the Heron, but soon they began to depart the way they came, vanishing through the chamber walls and ceiling like smoke up a flue.

The Heron lit on the back of a chair. Ogen stared at it in fear. He ripped open his shirt and saw that his chest was intact.

"Ogen."

Where the Heron had landed sat a spectral Herod. He

was bent and his face was crumbling. His robe was shabby. His crown had fallen into his lap. He was rotting away, kept intact by little more than Ogen's memory and devotion.

Ogen scrambled from the bedding and came to his knees before this vision.

"My king!"

"You doubt the magi."

"I have been faithful to your orders, my king. But they have dragged us all up and down Israel and found nothing."

"The little frogs."

"The little frogs went away! Jerusalem was unharmed and the people were amused! With respect, my king, those were signs, too!"

Herod angered. "I must *know*!"

"You shall know, my king. Even if I return the star men to you with nothing."

"My sons must *know*!"

"They shall, also."

"Return to me, Ogen."

"The star men cannot search forever, my king. I'll bring them before you either with their hands empty, or your orders done."

"My time is short."

"No, my king!"

Ogen threw his face to the floor. When he rose, the Heron once again stood on the chair. Herod's image had disappeared. The Heron flew to the window ledge and looked back at Ogen. It called *gaak*, raised its wings, and leaned out into the night.

Ogen picked up his wine cup emptied it into a basin.

CHAPTER 6

First Light

THE MAN REACHED down to the woman.

"It's time," he said.

She opened her eyes and held her arms up to him.

"We'll need to keep moving," he said, "but please don't be stubborn about stopping for rest."

The woman stood. "Stubborn? Me?"

They allowed themselves a short knowing laugh.

"It's tonight," she said.

"Did you dream it?"

"No." She picked up her bag.

"I see it," she said.

CHAPTER 7

The Travelers

SPRING WAS BEGINNING to threaten winter's grip on Judea. The nights were cold but the days warmed quickly. Sandar had been on the road from Jericho since before sunup. He had decided not to rest on the road; the anticipation of his visit to the house of Nathan in Jerusalem erased the weariness of his journey from Nazareth the day before and his early departure from Jericho. He had packed extra water, and bread and olive oil and beans, and a little cheese. And a little wine. From time to time he would close his dry cold eyes as he made his way through the rock pillars along the curving road. He wondered at yesterday's vivid vision of the familiar desert.

The road from Jericho to Jerusalem turned away from the Jordan, out of the valley and through the dry bleached-white hills of Judea, before reaching the more forested elevations. It would eventually come upon the Mount of Olives, sentinel to the Seven Hills of the capital. The twisting path cut off views ahead and behind, and a traveler frequently found himself alone on the road.

As Sandar and Zac rounded a bend, Sandar saw ahead of him two people on foot. From their dress, Sandar judged them to be a man and a woman. They were carrying little. The woman swayed when she walked; perhaps she was ill, or crippled. He would offer them food and drink. He watched as they disappeared around a curve.

The road straightened after the bend. He saw the man and woman up ahead, clearer now as he and Zac had closed the distance. The man had a pack on his back and carried a large and clumsy sack. The woman had a smaller sack. She appeared to be holding something against her body with her other hand, and walking gingerly with small steps. They did not speak to one another.

Two men, a fat one and a skinny one, ran out from behind a tall boulder toward the man and the woman.

"Zac, HIYEE!" Sandar shouted, and slapped the donkey hard on his flank. Zac did not like to gallop and was not often ordered to do so, but he knew when his quiet master made that sound and whacked his hindquarters, it was time to go. The big donkey dipped his rump and shoved off with his back legs and was at full speed in an instant.

They closed the distance to the crime in less than half a minute. The two robbers had heard Sandar's cry. The fat robber hurried to wrestle the man's sack away from him, but the man was resisting and held the robber's knife hand away while he fought to keep the sack. The skinny robber had snatched the woman's sack from her hand and had started back to the boulder.

Sandar brought Zac up between the skinny robber and the rock. He slid from the donkey and pulled a *gladius* and *makhaira* from scabbards he had hidden under his packs.

"It's Sandar the Giant!" the skinny robber hollered.

"I'm Sandar the Builder," Sandar said, "but I also take things apart. Drop the sack and that *sica*. I'm big but I saw you run and I'd catch you quickly and I say to you that you will drop them both because you'll have no hand to hold them with."

The skinny robber dropped the sack but kept the dagger and ran back past the rock and did not slow down as he disappeared over a hill and into the desert.

Sandar whirled to the traveler and the fat robber. The fat robber had the man in a bear hug from behind, and his dagger at his throat.

"I'll kill him!" the robber said. "Drop your sword and knife!"

Sandar snorted and raised his voice across the dozen cubits to the man and the fat robber. "I don't think you'll kill him in the moment before I reach you."

"I've killed stronger men than him!" the robber yelled. "And bigger men than you. Drop your weapons!"

Sandar walked almost casually to the two men, his weapons held loosely at his sides. He put his *makhaira* back into his belt, hoping to cool the confrontation, if only symbolically. He did not want to begin the shedding of blood. He noticed that the woman was calm; her face betrayed no hint of concern. He stopped three long strides away.

"I won't do that," Sandar said. "But I'll stop here and we can have a word."

"Drop your *gladius*! Stand away!"

Sandar said, "Perhaps you should consider –"

"I consider nothing! I'll kill him if you do not withdraw!"

"What advantage to you, since you'll be dead also, certainly after much suffering at my hands? You'll be even easier to catch than your partner. I'll leave your carcass unblessed for the vultures, or perhaps I'll leave you crippled and alive for the hyenas. A high price for sacks from a man without even a donkey."

"Silence! No more talking!"

Sandar said, "Two things to consider: First, compare the length of your legs, the size of your belly, and the reach of your blade, to mine. Second –"

He nodded to the man, who drove his elbow into the fat robber's stomach just below his heart and twisted away from him. Sandar rushed forward and kicked the fat robber hard in his genitals. The fat robber shrieked and rolled on the ground, gasping and crying loud tears.

"Do not kill him."

Sandar looked at the woman – barely a woman, but yes, Sandar saw, more than a girl. Certainly short of two decades on this earth. Her face was smooth and unsmiling under the shawl covering her head and drawn around her neck. But her voice was clear and strong, and unexpected after she had stood quietly observing the violence around her. Her bearing and voice were so out of the ordinary for young woman of Israel that her huge pregnancy was the last thing he noticed about her.

"I wouldn't wet my blade with him," Sandar said. He held his sword away from his body and lifted the still-bent robber to his feet by the neck of his tunic. "But perhaps we'll visit his own sacks." He turned to the man. "What's in your bags and pack, traveler?"

The man looked at the woman. "We have blankets, a few tools, some cloth for – for clothes," he said. "There is a little money for food along the way and to pay tax if we must. Some hard bread and as much water as we could carry. Two tunics, some inner garments, some pallets for sleep."

Now that Sandar was able to look him over more carefully, and from the sound of his voice, he could see that man himself was not much beyond adolescence.

Sandar pulled the still-bent fat robber to his feet. He was coughing and could barely speak. "What was the second?" he croaked.

"What?"

"The second thing to consider."

Sandar laughed. "Even a bandit should always protect his jewels." He began to drag the fat robber back to the boulder. "Come, we'll visit your own sacks behind the rock, eh? I'll be back shortly."

The woman raised her voice. "Bring us nothing. We will take nothing from this robber. We must go."

This was the second time Sandar was startled by a command from the young woman. He said again, slowly: "I'll be back shortly."

"Nothing," the man said, "we want nothing, we need nothing."

"We'll look, nevertheless," Sandar said. "I'll return and we'll have some food and drink and see what's what."

Behind the large rock Sandar found several bags and

a sad donkey tied to a tree. He threw the robber to the ground and waved the *gladius* at him. "You run and I'll finish you," he said. "I do not take orders from a girl."

Sandar looked from behind the rock back at the couple. "Will you take a donkey?" he called to them.

The man looked at the woman. She did not move or speak as she held her enormous belly.

"No," the man said.

Sandar shook his head and grunted. "Let's see what's in these sacks, eh, my swoll-balled friend?" Sandar said.

He found what he expected to find. Clothing, food. Household items, lamps. Some fine linens and silks, an embroidered shawl. Two donkey blankets.

"You left your victims little," Sandar said. The robber continued to whimper, curled up on the ground.

The second sack was large. In it he found a lake of coins; gold, silver, bronze. A third big bag was brimful of rubies and emeralds and precious stones of all kinds, and fine colored glass of every color; some loose, some set in rings and other jewelry. Sandar was shocked at the opulence sloshing around in those bags.

"You're a bad man but a good bandit," Sandar said. "I've never seen so much wealth in one place."

The fat robber struggled to sit up. "I worked very hard for those sacks," he said. "I wake up early and retire late."

"Some of this never traveled these roads," Sandar said. "Who did you rob?"

"Some, few," he said. Sandar looked up. "All right. Not just travelers. The wealthy in their homes. Please don't kill me. The girl said."

Sandar ignored his plea. "Money for the taxes. The Jews coming to their family centers to enroll for the assessments. Perhaps you robbed the collectors themselves. Maybe synagogues as well?"

"It's money," the fat robber said, starting to catch his breath, "or jewelry to turn into money. I don't care where it came from or why it was on this road or who it belongs to or where it was going."

Sandar said, "It's good that you don't care, because I'm going to take all of it."

"The girl said no," the robber said.

"I already told you, Sandar said. "The girl does not command me. Besides, since you have these riches through theft, they don't belong to you. Me having them is no less just than you having them, and if I take them your thieving will not have been rewarded. I'm known in Nazareth and some in Jerusalem, and I might be able to return some of this, especially the stones and jewelry. Now . . . ," Sandar said.

"Please don't kill me," the fat robber said. He had started to cry.

"Maybe I'll bind you across that nag of yours and take you with me to Jerusalem," Sandar said. "Let Herod's justice decide on mercy or none."

With that, the robber rolled over and sprang to his feet and limped away as fast as his tender groin would allow. Sandar had not seen any weapon in the sacks; between them the robbers only had one small dagger.

Sandar stuffed some cloth into each of the bags with the coins and jewelry to keep them quiet. He considered taking the donkey, but the poor animal was emaciated and old. Besides, the man and woman had rejected it and he had no use for it. He cut it loose to find food and water on its own.

When he emerged from behind the rock, the man had retrieved the girl's sack the skinny robber had dropped. When the man saw that Sandar was carrying something heavy, he said, "Please, no. We can take nothing."

Sandar shook his head. "I wouldn't burden you with this," he said. He secured the bags of coins and jewels in his own sacks across Zac's back. "But you'll allow me to offer bread and oil, and some of my water."

"First, we must thank you for your help," the man said. "You were most kind and brave. And your donkey is very fast." The man smiled. "Do you believe in the prophecies?" he asked.

"There are so many," Sandar said.

The young woman cleared her throat and glared pointedly at the man, who appeared to think better of that line of conversation.

"I'm Joseph," the man said. "This is Mary."

"I'm honored," Sandar said. He was struck by Joseph's words and Mary's interruption. Just the night before, at the Jericho tavern, the young astrologer had started to speak of prophecies and been cut off.

"And we are honored to be in the presence of Sandar the Builder," Joseph said.

"You know me?" Sandar said. "I'm known to many, but mostly in Nazareth," Sandar said.

"But I know Sandar the Builder well, by name and by

sight," Joseph said. "I'm a carpenter working in Nazareth. I recognize and admire many of your works."

"Ah, I'm doubly honored, then," Sandar said. He was a little surprised he had not encountered this workman from Nazareth before. "Are you a good carpenter?" he asked Joseph, a bit more bluntly than he had intended, and he chuckled to soften the question.

Mary said, "He is. He works in stone as well, with equal skill."

"You mentioned tools," Sandar said.

Joseph said, "One never knows when an encounter will lead to work. I'm as happy to be paid on the road as I am in Nazareth, should someone we encounter have a need."

"That's wise," Sandar said. He always carried basic tools himself when he traveled. "Will you be returning to Nazareth?"

"We don't know," Joseph said. "Much is uncertain for us. When we believe it's safe, yes, I believe we will return to Nazareth."

Sandar did not understand Joseph's words, and asked, "Why might you be unsafe, if even for some small period of time?"

"It is . . . a feeling," Mary said.

Sandar perceived that he had rescued a couple who were not of the ordinary, at least in their own minds, but he said to Joseph: "Please come to visit me when you return. With wood scarce, craftsmen in wood are scarce as well. Since you also have experience with stone, I'll have regular requirements you may be suited to meet. And perhaps I may intercede with those who are making trouble."

"Thank you," Mary said.

"Now, about that bread and water," Sandar said.

Mary said, "We thank you for your offer, but we must get to Bethlehem and we're now delayed by the bandits. We must decline your offer to pause any longer. God be with you." She turned to walk away and gestured for Joseph to join her.

"Bethlehem by tonight?" Sandar glanced at the sun. "At your slow pace you won't get through Jerusalem and on to Bethlehem at an hour that will allow you to find lodging. It's a small village with few places rest the night. Maybe none. Especially with your wife . . . ."

"We are betrothed," Joseph said. "We await the final ceremonies with our friends and families. When we return."

"Ah," Sandar said. Perhaps this circumstance gave rise to their fear of returning to Nazareth with a child appearing before the final celebrations. He nodded and considered how to turn his next words away from awkwardness, but at that moment a high glad feeling rose within him and when his words started, they came without thought, as if from another, and from an unknown place.

"I understand! Yes, betrothed, yes! But such a glorious thing to have come upon you!" he said. "Children are always a blessing. Always! God has favored you, pay no heed to the words of others, to the words of any, to the words of offices or titles, or even to the judgment of your own blood! Pay no heed to customs and laws, the old ways! God bless you all and accept my wishes for a safe arrival for the little one. You will visit me in Nazareth."

Mary and Joseph wondered at his words and the joy

behind them. Mary permitted herself a small, knowing smile. Sandar himself was shocked at the sound of what he had spoken; when his mind again became his he hoped his speech was not too forceful for the circumstances.

"Yes," Joseph said. "Well. We're . . . grateful to hear words of . . . understanding."

Mary said, "Your . . . your understanding is . . . rare. It matches your courage. We thank you for both."

The moment passed and Mary's sternness returned. "But your fine words don't get us closer to Bethlehem. We must go."

"Wait!"

"No! We're leaving now."

Sandar said, "It costs you not a second to indulge my companionship at least to Jerusalem. We can talk about Bethlehem on the way."

"I assure you there is nothing to talk about," Mary said.

Sandar turned to Joseph. "You don't rebuke your betrothed, addressing a man as she does?"

Joseph offered a wry smile. "I tried it. Once."

Sandar said, "I'm going to be with you anyway."

"We don't ask it or require it," Mary said.

"You do," Sandar said. "Turn around."

They turned to see the Lion standing atop a boulder, in profile.

Mary said, "Everyone knows lions do not attack people."

"Everyone except the ones they eat."

"Saving us does not give you license to mock me. I've never heard of people eaten by lions."

"Those people seldom return to report. The Persians didn't throw Daniel into the sheep's den!"

"God saved Daniel from the lions!"

"And God is showing us his ribs," Sandar said. "I won't leave you to discover why."

"Whatever he may crave, God has set our path," Mary said. "Join us if you feel you must. It changes nothing."

Joseph said, "Mary and I will welcome your protection and companionship to Jerusalem."

Sandar was grateful for Joseph's gesture towards calm. "If God is our guide, consider that God sent Zac, too. Whatever tonight's destination, you'll reach it more quickly if Mary rides, at least to Jerusalem."

Joseph looked at Mary and took a breath as if to speak. But he let his eyes tell Mary how he felt.

"After hauling me on his back from Nazareth," Sandar said, "Zac will be grateful."

The Lion switched its tail and disappeared behind the rock.

"I will ride," she said.

CHAPTER 8

The Magi Prepare

PEOPLE STOPPED IN the street to stare at the big horses with the beautiful blankets and the men dressed like kings. Was that a black king, that young one? The only horses they had ever seen had Rome's soldiers mounted, and even that was rare in Jericho. And those army horses were not so grand.

Ogen and his men were getting their donkeys and camels ready to travel. Ogen yelled at the boys who were along to wrangle the donkeys and camels and tend to the supplies. He slapped his fellow soldiers about their shoulders, urging them with false jocularity to shake off their hangovers from the night before. Some returned his laugh, some shook their heads and went through the motions of getting ready to ride.

The magi gathered in a group across the road where the big horses shielded them from Ogen and the guard.

Melchior addressed Balthazar: "Are you certain you know where the road splits to go south?"

The Egyptian smiled at his leader's nervousness. "Did you notice our hostler's young stablehand?"

"He's of your color. A countryman?"

"An Ethiope. The hostler purchased him out of slavery to apprentice."

"Ah," Old Caspar said. "You made his acquaintance."

"He was frightened of me at first," Balthazar said, "but we found some common words."

"Would one of those common words be 'Bethlehem'?" Old Caspar said.

"Another was 'silver,' which I happened to have in my hand. He has driven and retrieved animals to and from there. He assured me the fork is obvious and described the landmarks in some detail."

"Let's hope he didn't befriend Ogen," Melchior said.

"Herod's guard can hardly bear to look at me," Balthazar said, "and the stablehand hides when they're about."

"Busy yourselves," Melchior said. Ogen approached.

Ogen said: "A fine day for king-hunting, eh, Melchior? Perhaps my men can assist you in looking behind rocks on the Jerusalem road."

"Spare me your sarcasm, Ogen."

Ogen laughed unconvincingly. "None intended, my leader! The sooner you find this mysterious child, the sooner my men and I may return to the palace and to Herod."

"Really, Ogen? You seemed to enjoy yourself hugely at the tavern last night. At Herod's expense, I might add."

Ogen waved off the insult. "These stars of yours – or perhaps whatever has hopped out of the swamp – do they predict a small boy on a tiny throne wearing a tiny crown? Or a newborn spouting the Torah? Perhaps a sword-swinging toddler leading an army of infants with daggers in their swaddle?"

Old Caspar said, "What must life be like for you, Ogen, with no imagination? Of course the stars don't point to particular places or persons. Our search is a great adventure! Come, man, let your heart be open!"

Ogen clutched at his chest and his manner darkened.

"So you confess your task is purely one of imagination! My life? My life is to be loyal to the real tasks Herod sets for me."

"I'm comforted to hear that, Ogen," Old Caspar said. "You may now display your loyalty to the real task of hoisting me up on this horse."

A shadow flickered over them. Ogen watched the Heron light on the stable roof.

"What bird is that?" he asked.

"A heron," Balthazar said.

"WHAT?"

One of the soldiers had come up to speak to Ogen. "A heron. They feed and nest along the Jordan."

"You need to get out of Jerusalem more often," Balthazar said.

Ogen stared at the Heron. He felt at his chest again.

"Amos!" he said. "Levi! Come assist Old Caspar with his mount."

He turned to the magi. "Your time is running out," he said.

CHAPTER 9

The Plan

SANDAR THOUGHT ABOUT the three astrologers he had met at the tavern. Perhaps they were meant to see and feel the living sky and stones he had experienced the day before. Would they see the world glow as he did, and would they recognize it as the sign they sought and read it to their purpose?

He considered mentioning to Mary and Joseph his experience on the same road they had taken from Nazareth. But his relations with them felt fragile, despite Mary's grudging acceptance of his company to Jerusalem; he thought it best not to give the impression that he was a man who saw unlikely things.

The route through the rugged hills was a steady climb, but Sandar was strong and Joseph was young and Zac the donkey, bearing Mary, was indifferent to the rising road.

Sandar walked ahead of them at a brisk pace to encourage an arrival in Jerusalem as soon as possible, and to give them some privacy. Joseph stayed close to Mary to steady her as she sat on Zac, her legs to one side. They spoke infrequently to one another in low tones; it sounded like Joseph was inquiring as to how Mary was feeling. Mary's answers were brief and soothing.

"Your donkey's gait is smooth," Joseph called out. "We're thankful for that."

So Joseph wished to speak. Sandar slowed to let them catch up. "Zac is a blessing to his rider," Sandar said. "His longer stride has eased my way all over these lands, and I'm sure he's honored to bear Mary this day."

"May I ask what draws you to Jerusalem?" Joseph said.

Sandar did not know why he hesitated to answer Joseph's question. Many of his friends knew of his mission, and Joseph and Mary were agreeable enough companions, with no stake in what he did or did not do.

Mary said, "You are hoping to know your path upon the world."

Sandar was surprised at Mary's words. She spoke as though she . . . knew things, and indeed, she knew this thing.

"Yes," he said, "yes. You speak poetically, but truthfully. Hoping to know my path, or hoping to make it."

Joseph chuckled. "I never seem to know what's going on."

"You will find it," Mary said.

There was no reason to keep his mission from this woman, stern though she may be, and her betrothed. "It's time, it's past time, for me to take a wife. I regret I've let business distract me from this, this – it's a duty, is it not, as well as a pleasure? A man who knows my family, and from whom I've purchased decorations for my buildings, has a daughter. I'm meeting him – them – at his home Jerusalem. I hope she will agree to marry."

"Me, that is," Sandar laughed.

"It's not certain?" Joseph said.

Sandar said, "Although her father has indicated his strong approval – more than that, his strong desire – to part with his daughter for my benefit, I'll require her consent. I don't keep slaves."

"You haven't met her," Joseph said.

Sandar said, "Perhaps I'm arrogant, but I'm hopeful that the prospect of a marriage with me – I'm not unfair of figure, and my prospects are more than fair – will make for a courtship that will begin and end with our meeting, as the tradition has come to be."

Joseph said, "I'm certain you'll succeed. But your voice betrays concern."

"She's a strong woman?" Mary said. "Perhaps difficult with suitors?"

Sandar thought: *She phrased her response as questions to deflect the impression of secret knowledge.* He pretended not to notice.

"I've heard this from Jerusalem friends who know the family," Sandar said, "and her father has suggested the same. The truth is, I'll be pleased to have a strong woman and it it's why my interest in the maidens of Nazareth has to date been small."

He instantly realized the implied insult. "I'm sorry," he said, "I didn't mean – "

Mary laughed. "I'm quite immune from offense among the maidens of Nazareth. The maids, the women, want little to do with me."

"Also," Sandar said, "it's said she's comely, and both unusually tall and fair, as am I among the Jews."

"You're not Jewish," Mary said.

This Mary, Sandar thought. For better or worse, she speaks her thoughts.

"The priests report that my father was Roman and my mother Greek. Also, as you see" – Sandar played with a bit of his blond hair – "sometime in the past a Northman got over the wall."

"There are Jews with your color," Mary said.

"Aye, but few of my height and size and . . . I regret that my profile is" – he laid a finger aside of his nose – "undistinguished."

Joseph said, "You face a challenging courtship."

"I was raised by devout Jewish parents and I continue to honor them and their faith. I hope the daughter of Nathan will not reject me for my blood."

"And if her tongue is sharp?" Mary said.

"I've heard this as well," Sandar said. "But I'm a worker of wood and stone and clay. I'm accustomed to sharp things, and slow to anger. I require only that she perform the offices of a wife and –" He paused; he was making her sound like the slave he said she was not.

"And mother," Mary said.

"If God should bless us," Sandar said. "And that she show me respect in my house, which I'll return. And affection, if I've earned it, and which I'll also return. And," he smiled at Mary, "I'll welcome guidance of the sort that men sometimes require."

Mary said, "Builder Sandar, you will have the love of many children. Your own love is great and will be returned."

Sandar was becoming accustomed to the odd but serene sureness in Mary's speech, even as little as he understood it. "I'll be happy with one," Sandar said. "The truth is, the daughter would be coming to marriage later than usual for her people, as am I, although by all signs she is possessed of a hearty good health and capable of childbearing."

"Your children will be of size," Joseph said. "You'll need an even bigger donkey."

Sandar laughed his strong chest-deep laugh. "It would be my pleasure to find seven more like good Zac here, should our family require it."

"But first . . . ," Joseph said.

"Aye, Joseph," Sandar said. "First she must make a marriage with me." Sandar was once again embarrassed at the implication of his words in front of the couple yet to complete the marriage customs. But Joseph showed no reaction, and Mary nodded.

"How is she called?" Joseph said.

"Susannah, only child of Nathan and Miriam," Sandar said.

"Ah," Joseph said, "the lily. A tall strong flower. Let's hope her judgment is as quick as her words. God be with you in your task."

Sandar looked at Mary sitting steadily on Zac as the three of them continued through the hills. Joseph and Mary were an unusual pair. To the eye they seemed poor and fragile. If he had not overtaken them along the way they might both be dead and their unborn along with them, or at least robbed of their goods. At the same time they displayed resolution and strength, demanding of themselves that they achieve Bethlehem before another sunrise for some reason sufficient to themselves.

"Have you thought again about your need to reach Bethlehem tonight?" Sandar said. "It would honor me to assist you with lodging in Jerusalem. In fact, I would insist."

"Oh," Joseph said. "We haven't questioned our destination as Bethlehem tonight."

"Lodging in Bethlehem is uncertain, if there's any at all," Sandar said, "especially as you'll be arriving after close of day at the earliest, and almost certainly well after nightfall. And it's David's town; many Jews claim through him. Many must have been going there for the census and tax. It's barely a town. You don't even carry a tent."

"We thank you," Joseph said, "and we have considered the difficulties but they –"

"They are not difficulties," Mary said.

"You'll not make Bethlehem tonight with any hope of shelter. Please allow –"

"No! Welcome as your assistance has been, we didn't seek it. We don't seek it now. Please don't force your charity on us."

"But why did you set out for Bethlehem now, with Mary's time so close? What's so important about tonight, and Bethlehem?"

"Unlike you," Mary said, "we are without the means to be away from Nazareth for a day more than is necessary."

Oop – she's forgotten their story. A little while ago they told me they might not even return to Nazareth. What are they keeping from me, and why?

Sandar was wearying of challenging their obsession with Bethlehem, and with reaching it that night. And the couple had encountered enough trouble for the day, the desert and the robbers, and Mary's condition through it all. He was reluctant to add to their discomfort with an argument they seemed unwilling to concede. But he was stubborn, too, and not accustomed to defeat. He was not ready to give up trying to steer their resolve to something more sensible.

So Mary now claims it's a matter of "means"? All right. "That's why I'm offering –"

"Listen!" Joseph said.

A thin mewing sound rose from the brush. Sandar walked to the roadside and parted the weeds. It was a little Fox, lying on its side, dying, agitated as its waning moments allowed. It was emaciated; its coat was poor and its eye cloudy.

"A Fox," Sandar said. "Very young. Its pack has left it behind to die."

Sandar returned to Zac for a bag of water.

"We can't save it, Builder," Joseph said. "We must be –"

Mary touched Joseph's shoulder.

Sandar said, "No living thing should suffer, even at the end." He wet a cloth and, holding the Fox's head up, squeezed water into its mouth. The Fox lapped to catch as much as it could, and quieted. As Sandar stroked the Fox's coat, his eyes moistened.

"Go to sleep, little one," he said. "Your morning will be here soon."

Sandar rose slowly and returned to Mary and Joseph. "You're right. I may only have prolonged his end. Let's go."

Mary's eyes softened.

Sandar himself wanted to calm matters. "We shouldn't be arguing. Please help me understand –"

Joseph: "Sandar!"

They turned to see the little Fox trotting along behind them. His eyes were bright; his coat shone. The travelers stopped. The Fox sat.

"He's no threat," Mary said. "Zac doesn't seem to mind. Let him join our little band."

Joseph said. "That Fox was one minute from dead."

Sandar looked for a long moment back at the panting little Fox and shook his head. He said, "Perhaps it's a sign for us to renew our good feelings."

"We should," Joseph said, "but our need to be in Bethlehem tonight is not a matter of our feelings, or yours."

Sandar shook his head and allowed himself a slight chuckle. "All right. All right. I'm sorry I spoke sharply; I'm too used to giving orders. I suppose it really isn't necessary for me to understand why you travel now, why tonight is –"

Suddenly, he did understand, yet did not.

"You wish to be delivered in Bethlehem."

"Yes," Mary said.

"That's meaningful to you?"

"It is . . . beyond understanding," Mary said.

Sandar laughed and raised his hands in surrender. "Finally, we agree."

Joseph said, "You're right about the Jews going to Bethlehem. I'm of David's house, through Solomon and Josiah and Eliud and many others over the several hundred-years. Jacob of Nazareth is my father."

"There is no benefit to you in Herod's taxation nor in Rome's for the child to be born in Bethlehem. You risk giving birth on the road, perhaps before your time." He saw that Mary was about to speak, but he raised his hand to stop her. "But perhaps our Fox friend reminds me there is much that must remain mysterious. I can't resist what I don't understand, and so . . . ."

Joseph looked at his betrothed. Despite their hardships, and surely more to come, he was calm. As was Mary; there seemed to be a pact between them that called for serenity in the face of all of their challenges.

"Your kindnesses we will always remember," Mary said. "But we ask you most earnestly not to be troubled about our plans."

"Too late for that," Sandar said. "I ask you to listen to a plan of my own."

"Your plans and ours are likely to remain at odds. At Jerusalem we will bid you –"

Joseph touched Mary to be still. "The Builder has heard our decision but he has earned our ears."

"My business with Nathan and Susannah will likely be short, for better or worse," Sandar said. "We've made good time on the road and should achieve the Mount of Olives within the hour and the city right after. That will put us there some time before sundown. There's a place near the market you can rest. I'll leave you food and water. You're both at the limits of your endurance and without food and rest, Bethlehem tonight will remain a dream."

The couple's silence spoke their understanding.

"Your rest was interrupted in Jericho last night," Sandar said.

"You saw us," Joseph said. "That was you."

Sandar nodded. "After I have Susannah's answer, we'll travel to Bethlehem together. Even with a stop in Jerusalem, you'll reach Bethlehem sooner with Mary riding Zac and me setting the pace on foot."

Joseph said, "In our dreams, we walk alone into what awaits us."

"And yet – here I am. I understand the power of dreams. But no dream, no part of your destiny, no – no *story* – of which you believe yourselves to be a part, requires you to reject assistance at this most difficult and dangerous of times for you and your little one. I'll escort you out of Jerusalem and to Bethlehem and – and you will sleep in Bethlehem tonight."

Mary took a deep breath.

"Tonight, and until your time," Sandar said, "whenever that is visited upon you."

Joseph said to Mary, "Our dreams must not be selfish," but the answer would be hers.

"It would be welcome to find some shade and recline for a bit," she said. "And it's so, I am hungry. And," she added, "we'll want to hear the good news of your meeting with Susannah."

"The courtship may be brief," Sandar said.

Mary turned to Joseph. "Our friend Sandar the Builder

is become part of our journey" – she nodded to Sandar – "our *story*. I will not be early delivered because we allowed ourselves rest for a while in Jerusalem, or because he has offered his aid to what must be."

She turned to Sandar. "I know we may seem difficult to you. But we're grateful beyond words for your grace."

"Yes," Joseph said. "I'm not a man of words but my heart overflows with thanks."

"Very well, very well," Sandar said. Now that they had agreed, he was a bit embarrassed that he had gotten his way with these two poor and simple people who, for all that, seemed to walk in mystery. "It's I who owe you both thanks for making this journey one of meaning for me." He laughed quietly. "No matter what Susannah says."

And whatever that meaning might be, he thought.

"Zac thinks it's a good idea too, don't you boy? And what about our little friend?"

Sandar turned to look behind them but the Fox had disappeared.

What must be?

CHAPTER 10

Susannah

"Sandar! A thousand welcomes! A great day for my household!" Nathan was a small man and could barely get his arms around Sandar. "You're looking well and even after your dusty journey your continued prosperity is apparent."

"I'm pleased to be here," Sandar said. He glanced around his host's home. He recognized a table he had made for Nathan to commemorate their many successful dealings. "Is Miriam about?"

"Miriam very much supports this union," Nathan said, "but she's sad to think that Susannah will live in Nazareth and was fearful that her eyes might influence this meeting. She has taken her tears to visit friends."

"You speak of Susannah's consent as though it had been accomplished," Sandar said. "That wasn't something I had been led to expect."

"Ach," Nathan said, "how could she refuse? Yes, she turned down some in her youth – and more recently – but

I've taken steps with our local priest. I've assured him of your devotion despite your birth, and have guaranteed his approval with a pledge of increased support. And he has promised Miriam that her daughter's marriage to a man raised in the shadow of the synagogue by believers will be blessed, despite the blood of your ancestors."

"I'm pleased to have your priest's blessing," Sandar laughed, "whatever his intercession in my favor may cost you." He grew serious. "But I don't seek his company. My aim here is to gain the hand of your daughter, and perhaps even her heart."

"Yes, yes, of course," Nathan said. "But it never hurts to have the priest throw in an extra prayer, perhaps even whisper in Susannah's ear should she require further persuasion."

"It's unusual to marry outside the tribe," Sandar said. "But in some respects I'm a man without a tribe. I hope that won't displease Susannah."

Nathan lowered his voice. "I know Susannah's manner has become known to you," he said. "It's not always easy to know what will displease her. To be blunt, I thought a Gentile-by-birth might appeal to her contrariness." He paused, fearful he had painted his daughter uninvitingly. "Um, perhaps 'contrariness' isn't the right word. I meant it in the sense of 'adventuresome nature.'"

Sandar laughed. "I knew what you meant. Perhaps I should mention to you that I've brought the *mohar*." He placed a leather drawstring bag on the table. "It reflects the honor I feel. I hope you will regard it as sufficient."

"Uch," Nathan said. "Please, put it away. Regard it as my gift to my daughter. This union is, shall we say, unconventional on account of her years and yours, and your parentage, so let's not be too stern about the old customs. I can assure you Susannah has little interest in them." He shrugged. "Ha, she has never honored them!"

Nathan remembered something. "You and I, we're men of business and I expect we'll continue our dealings whatever today's outcome."

"Certainly, my friend."

"I treasure that as I will treasure the joining of our families. Not that Susannah is without value to Miriam and me, but . . . ."

"But it's time," Sandar said. "Time for me, too. Past time."

Sandar was not certain what to expect. Whenever he formed an image of Susannah in his mind, he would dismiss it as based on nothing, no information other than impressions from Nathan and their mutual acquaintances, whose favorable reports had about them some faintness of enthusiasm, and who could not disguise their idea that Susannah, whatever merits she might offer, possessed a distinctive flavor of a piquancy perhaps not suited to all tastes.

Nathan said, "If I may put a smile on matters, her . . . choices have left her available for you here now. Had she been more . . . compliant with my wishes in the past she would be married to one of several worthy young men I selected for her."

A woman's voice said, "Two of those worthy young men left this house in tears."

Susannah had appeared in the doorway to the back rooms. Sandar stood and beheld a woman the likes of whom he had not imagined existed in the lands he traveled. She was tall and not at all stout as he had surmised, but broad of shoulder. She wore a white tunic of rich fabric that reached the floor with two stripes of brightly-colored embroideries down its length. She broadcast an impression of strength and sturdiness beneath an undeniable womanliness.

Her features were large and strong; her mouth full but unsmiling. Her complexion was fairer than that of any woman he could remember. Her height did not match his, but her gaze sought his face directly and without modesty. Her eyes were clear but not the brown of the country; blue? No, grey, light grey.

She wore no covering on her head and her hair was unplaited, falling to her shoulders in soft waves. It was the color of flax and ash.

"I go uncovered in my own house," she said. "You need to see me."

Sandar was suddenly aware that he had not removed the cap he had worn in the bright sun. He swept it off his head.

"I am Sandar," he said. "I'm honored to meet you."

"I will retire," Nathan said.

"Please stay, father," she said. She looked Sandar over from toe to head. "I heard you were also fair. And you're beardless, I see."

Sandar did not know what courtly strategy to employ with this woman of reputed touchiness. He decided that putting on the weeds of a less forthright man would be dishonest and easily detected. She appeared to be ready to converse with some candor.

"We both stand out among our countrymen," he said.

"You're also large, as told to me," she said. "You needn't say anything about my size or my color. I'm well aware of both."

"I've found my size to be advantageous," Sandar said. "Just today I stopped an attack by robbers on the road from Jericho."

"Did you kill them?"

"I drove them off."

"How many?"

"Two."

"They were foolish to try to rob you."

"In truth, I came upon them trying to rob a man and a woman on the road. My donkey and I interrupted their attack and my *gladius* spoke with its customary eloquence."

"You share credit with your donkey," she said. "That's admirable."

"He's an admirable donkey," Sandar said.

Susannah said, "How many donkeys do you have?"

"Only Zac."

"Ah, for Zacharias," she said. "'God remembers.' Let us hope so."

"God surely does, but it's only Zac."

"It's a very . . . manly name."

"I selected it for its sound, simple but sudden out of the throat to get his attention. He seems to know it when I speak to him. He's not a donkey inclined to put on airs with a fancy name."

"One donkey does not suggest you foresee a successful outcome to your suit here today."

"It suggests nothing of the sort, my lady, as I've already arranged with the hostler to purchase another should my journey become our journey, if fortune smiles and God wills."

Susannah looked at him with interest.

"You are bold."

"I see no reason not to acknowledge that I'm here for you, if you will have me."

She looked at Nathan. "Father has told you I've demanded a voice in my marriage."

"And I would not have a woman who came to me unwillingly," Sandar said, "or, for that matter, less than completely willingly and without some enthusiasm. You're free to reject me, or to accept me on conditions you may yourself propose and that I'll consider fairly. But I must hear your answer today."

"You speak well," she said, "and your words are pleasing, if stronger than a maid is likely to hear."

"Words mean nothing unless the heart perceives their truth. But you're kind to say so."

"I'm not accustomed to being told I am kind."

"I'm certain you're not accustomed to many things that life with me will present to you," Sandar said.

"You presume much."

"I do not presume failure," Sandar said. "I believe I'm a fair match for you and you for me. Of course, let's be forthright with one another: I've heard of your disposition. But I believe your care in judging suitors isn't just a woman's normal caution, but is born of your heart's demand for a life like no other, a life of wonder and searching."

Susannah's eyes widened; there was a touch of fear in them.

"That's also my heart's demand," Sandar said.

Susannah was startled into silence. This large fair smooth-faced man, a stranger to her, had spoken truly. She had not yet offered a smile or any warmth of welcome.

"In these few minutes you've come to know my heart?"

"I don't wish to presume to read your heart. But I'm wondering if perhaps the worthy young men your father mentioned measured worthiness in a way that was not . . . meaningful to you."

"And how do you measure your own worthiness in my eyes?" Susannah tossed her head to shake back some locks that had fallen across her face, which gesture, she was pleased to feel, restored the feeling of imperiousness with which she was comfortable when speaking with hopeful suitors, but of which this man had taken no notice.

Sandar ignored the question. "It excites me that you hold my eye. I'm accustomed to maids casting their gaze downward when we speak."

"There is nothing on the ground that interests me," Susannah said.

"Yes! Exactly!" Sandar said. You've spoken my very mind! The narrow paths of the earth – there must be more for us!"

Susannah was startled at Sandar's insight. Her defenses flared.

"You are not Jewish," she said.

"I was raised in the faith and practice it, perhaps not as fervidly as some, but with all honor to the patriarchs and to my Jewish parents who adopted me and raised me and, I'm certain, loved me and love me still. I'm acquainted with the prophets – perhaps better acquainted than some of your, our, tribe – and I sometimes sit with the priests to hear their words. I pray to learn what God desires of us, no less than you and your ancestors."

"But you're not of the blood."

"I must presume to say, that doesn't sound like the woman of independent mind I was told to expect. I guarantee were we each to open a vein right now you would see no difference in the blood that would spill. In all ways that matter I'm as Jewish as you are."

"I've never been spoken to like that," she said.

"That pleases me," Sandar said. "As I told you a moment ago, you have much new to look forward to."

"The priests would never accept that argument," she said, "and neither do I."

"I know," Sandar said, and he threw his head back and laughed. Susannah was not expecting this merry reaction to her accusation, and she shuffled a half-step back from him.

"You're right, of course," he said. "The blood of the old ones does not run through me. If you deem that purely worldly circumstance sufficient cause for rejection, then you and I may deem our business concluded."

It was a risk. Sandar took it. He picked up his cap and turned to the door, reaching for the *mohar*. Nathan reached out his arm to delay Sandar's leaving.

Susannah started forward and raised her voice:

"I didn't say that."

Sandar smiled at the door he was now facing.

"Perhaps I misheard," he said.

He was thoroughly enjoying these ripostes with this unusual woman. Not another one like her in Galilee. Not Judea either, and almost certainly not Samaria. A quiet joy came upon him.

More.

He was in love.

Susannah's alarm had faded, but she was not through resisting this man who did not speak like the hopeful young men Nathan had brought to her, not even those educated for the priesthood. "There's a bag on the table I don't recognize as of this house. Is that my *mohar*?"

"It was going to be," Sandar said.

"How much am I worth?"

"Your father refused it."

"He was going to give me away for nothing?" Susannah said. "He was so anxious to rid the household of me?"

"And if he had accepted my offering," Sandar said, his face full of smiles, "you would have complained that you were being treated as a chattel to be bought and sold! Do not deny it, daughter of Nathan!" He laughed.

"It's a rather small bag," she said, unsmilingly, but with a melodramatic lilt. She picked up the bag and shook it. "And it doesn't make much noise. I would have urged father to hold out for a better price. After all," she continued, fighting back a smile, "I'm larger than the usual daughter, and offer excellent value."

"Had your father found my offer wanting, I would gladly have haggled with him for your hand." Sandar laughed again, more heartily this time, now certain that

Susannah was making a joke. "I might have been willing to throw a goat or two into the deal. Perhaps an ox to be identified at a later date."

Susannah dipped her head and her eyes smiled at him under her brow.

"Jokes aside, should Nathan have demanded the *mohar*, I would gladly have bargained with him for a heavier bag, as I'm certain my credit is good with him." Nathan nodded, now a bit sad that he had so hastily declined Sandar's gold. "Besides," Sandar said, "I daresay you could walk out of this household any time you wanted without recompense to your father. And if you were inclined to do so, why not do it with me? Even in our brief conversation here, I think we have come to know one another quite well."

"Your boldness is both refreshing and offensive," Susannah said. "I don't know which odor is stronger."

"I regret I'm a bit ripe from the road."

"As long as we're being bold, let us discuss this frankly," she said. "We are not young among those who marry. I'm set in my ways, and I perceive that you're a man of accomplishment and most likely set in yours. How can we agree to wed knowing so little?"

"Of what value do you consider your 'ways,' as you call them?" Sandar said. "I will tell you I value mine almost not at all. What have those ways yielded me? A life of lonely labor which will only change when it ends. A life traveling this little patch of Israel with my tools, scrabbling for worthy workmen and my next engagement. And, in the middle of all of it, wondering why I'm here, wondering why the large earth and endless sky and the world of learning and thought and feeling are closed to me, why my feet must seek the same roads, day in and day out.

"Rewards of the world have come my way, yes. Yet here I am, my arms and home open before you, wanting something more and better, wanting to know what will truly please God. You want something more and better, too, or you would not have judged your prior suitors, who I suspect were conventional young men of business in Jerusalem, with such a fierce eye.

"I mean no offense to my great friend Nathan, but what ways within these walls do you seek to preserve?"

Susannah marveled at Sandar's easy speech. She had given up trying to match it. "My life here . . . father . . . mother . . ."

"I honor them both," Sandar said, "but these walls are the story of their lives, not yours – certainly not ours."

He waited for her response.

He had met all of her objections.

She has to be thinking. She can't just stand there saying nothing.

It struck him for the first time that he was facing a judge who had convicted many but, in the case before him, did not know how to decide. He could not let this pause continue; it made it too easy for her to bid him a safe return to Nazareth. Like potential clients who had to decide whether to engage his services, she needed to hear his final offer. Time to fill this silence with his best case.

He said, "I'm prepared to cast my ways aside, or as many of them as necessary to make a life with you. Oh, I'll continue to build, as I must provide for you and will do so with pleasure. And I would expect you to make our home in the ways customary for women of Galilee and Judea. Yes, I would expect that.

"I'll set aside rooms in the house that you will require for yourself, or build more for your use. We'll participate in the life of the synagogue or not, as you wish. We'll visit Nathan and Miriam frequently and welcome them in our home, and we'll lodge them with us in their later years if they require it.

"Perhaps I have not exhausted the 'ways' in which you feel you're 'set' that you fear will be unhappily interrupted. I'm certain that as persons no longer children we can make our way through them.

"I should add another thing, although I suspect this may mean little to you. As my wife you'll be a prominent woman in Galilee, much honored and respected. You're accustomed to using your voice in this house; you won't be deprived of that as my wife, and it will sound beyond our walls.

"And as for the rest – let me tell you: I do not expect to rule you. I do not expect to decide for our lives without your advice and agreement, and quite possibly, a lively dispute. Eh? We'll enjoy that, as we're enjoying ourselves right now."

"Are we?" Susannah said.

Sandar dropped his voice. "Otherwise you would already have dismissed me."

Sandar thought: *Where did these fine words and thoughts come from? I have never spoken so and yet they poured out as though I were not their author. Strange as they sounded in my voice, they fit exactly my cause: I can hardly portray a more attractive life for this delightfully haughty princess of Jerusalem.*

Susannah understood that this man, this Sandar, this Builder, had evaded all of her defenses, except the ones he had knocked down entirely. Nathan was smiling; he sensed she had weakened.

But she had not surrendered.

"Let me return to one of your fine phrases," she said. "You say you will need to provide for *me*."

Sandar rejoiced that she was still talking. "I'll speak truthfully: I would like a child, children if God wills it."

"I would not be young among Jerusalem's brides. If I am barren?"

Even at this unhappy thought, Sandar's heart was glad. *She is accepting the thought of children of our bodies.*

"I myself was adopted," Sandar said. "There are many worthy children who need love and support and instruction in the ways of the world. And, may God forbid it, who can know of my own seed? Ha! Perhaps we'll be as Sarah and Abraham, but let's not be concerned about children – they will come if they come. Know this: my love and my loyalty to you will be without conditions."

"Love?" Susannah said. "That's a word foreign to this conversation so far."

"Let us introduce it," Sandar said.

"You're prepared to love me based on this brief interview?" she said. "Forever?" She allowed a smile to overcome her reserve.

Perhaps I'm fooling myself, but that did not sound mocking; it sounded flirtatious.

"Before I entered the home of Nathan today, I had hoped to make a marriage with a willing woman. Nothing more. You know that I was told you were difficult, I do not deny it, and I was prepared to accept it. But I'm excited to find that it's not true. You're lively and quick. You don't speak sharply, only with care. You're not angry, only direct. You have disputed with men not accustomed to disputing with women and now, with you before me, I see their reports mean nothing."

She did not respond, as she believed this about herself.

"Perhaps . . . perhaps that's why your beauty has been unjustly neglected in accounts."

Nathan said, "Susannah, my daughter . . . ," but she raised her hand gently for him to stop.

Sandar said, "I'll speak of love, and offer it, if you will be with me. I need know nothing more of you to ask you – you, not your father – for your life as my wife."

"Sandar, called the Builder," she said. He liked the way it sounded when she said it; there was music in it. "I confess I'm surprised at you. I had expected a rough man with unrefined ways."

"And there will be times when your expectations will likely be met," he said. "But I say to you that I will never raise my hand to you or behave in a way that will bring shame on our house or that of Nathan and Miriam. I'm a man of steady habits and sober. I like to laugh and I like to make others laugh and you'll discover your own ribs pleasurably aching from time to time, I'm quite certain."

They looked at each other. Sandar could not tell if anything at all was passing between them. Her guard was high;

very high, still. But her face was a mask, and her smile had not returned. A shade had come over her eyes, and she had started to blink. After the few warm moments, she seemed to be slipping away.

"It . . . it's so soon," she said.

"Ach," Nathan said, "the young ones, their marriages are arranged for them and they go off together with almost no meeting at all. Your mother and I – "

"I honor my mother but I am not her, and, father, whom I also honor, you are assuredly not the Builder Sandar. And we've observed that I'm neither a young one nor one subject to being assigned a mate," she said. "Marriage to this man – I beg your pardon for speaking of you thus in your presence – marriage to you, Sandar, called the Builder – fresh from the road, just appearing at our door like a peddler, I . . . ."

"Then let us be betrothed, Susannah." Sandar said. It was the first time he had used her name. It filled his heart to hear his voice say it. "Come with me now. See me in the world, and I will see you, and we'll see one another together. I pledge to you in the presence of your father Nathan that I will not dishonor you, I will not force myself on you in any way during this time. You will have lodging for yourself in Nazareth during this time, and then we'll decide – *we* will decide, together – whether our friends will join us for the wedding celebration and march to my – to our home."

Susannah was breathing heavily. "You have achieved the rare success of leaving me with no ready response."

"You risk nothing," Sandar said.

Once again, Sandar felt the need to fill the silence between them.

"Let me tell you something while you ponder my proposition in your heart," Sandar said. "I mentioned that I assisted a man and woman on the road to Jerusalem from Jericho today. Joseph and Mary are waiting for me now. The woman is large with child and may be only days, perhaps even hours, from giving birth. They're betrothed but without the benefit of ceremony so far. An unusual pair who seem to believe they're living a story of their own, but – there is something about them. I've taken a liking to them. Perhaps I'm a fool in this hard world, but they seem poor and helpless and I may assist them with little cost or delay. I escorted them to Jerusalem and have promised to escort them to Bethlehem this evening, as they are insisting for reasons of their own that she be delivered there.

"There is no conclusion to this story; I just wanted you to know that our life together will start with the adventure I have promised – a journey this night to Bethlehem, without knowing what we'll find when we arrive. Or what . . . difficulties under the moon tonight.

"So I ask you again, and I'll ask you again after that, and again until I hear the answer my heart craves:

"Will you come with me now? Be my betrothed to be held apart from me until we're wed by ceremony. I believe you will find me worthy even if you're not prepared to find me so today."

Her breath had begun to come in gulps, and her eyes were brimming. "Father," she said.

"Susannah, my daughter, my only," Nathan said. "Go

with this good man. He is known to me and many others to be honorable and regular in his dealings and he has sworn his intentions before me, your father."

"I feel he is," she said. "A good man, and honorable. But I – I can't – so soon – our fathers' blood –"

Sandar said, "I'm a simple man. I stand before you with empty hands but a heart you've filled in just our few moments together. The blood is nothing. The blood is nothing! Susannah, I need – you need –"

"You are not a simple man." She was barely able to get the words out.

"My love is simple," he said.

"Oh, my father!" The words were difficult.

She turned and ran from the room, crying.

"Susannah!" Nathan called after her.

Even as Susannah's interest had seemed to grow as the interview continued, Sandar had already seen that she would reject him – rather, reject the idea of going with him as women were expected to go with men selected for them.

He now reached out and touched the arm of Nathan's robe. "I pleaded my best suit," he said, "and my only one. Susannah is much more than promised. Nathan, you have raised a woman to reckon with, an extraordinary woman, you and Miriam. But I have my answer and I must go to my friends."

"Perhaps . . . the priest . . . Miriam . . . . "

Sandar's words emerged with care. "I know what I need to know," he said. "She knows what she needs to know. I won't return to say the same things I said today. Plainly, they have upset her – the last result I wished for your good daughter.

"Several maids of Galilee, rather, their fathers, await my return. They are unlikely to flee, and the *mohar* will greatly assist their households. Those negotiations will be simple, if not so intriguing.

"I need to return to Joseph and Mary. Yes, my friend, we'll continue to have dealings in our businesses. We need not speak further of today. Your courtesies are much appreciated and I'm honored to have been a guest in your home and a suitor invited for your only child. I ask that you convey my great respect to Miriam along with regrets that we were not met on this visit."

He replaced his cap, picked up the *mohar*. He leaned to embrace Nathan and said, "May God bless this house with a successful suitor."

Sandar walked out into the late afternoon sun. The day was beginning to cool. He could hear sobbing from the depths of the house.

CHAPTER 11

Miracles at the Market

THE SUN GREW heavy over the hills of Jerusalem.

It seemed to mock Sandar's own heart as it dimmed and reddened and sank. But he had known that his task at the house of Nathan would be difficult and might fail. Now that it had, he allowed himself a short period of regret as he made his way back to the stable to retrieve Zac and settle with the hostler. The regret was intense, but he did not fight it, wanting it to eat its way out of him and depart.

The image that had been created of Susannah was not false by the lights of those who created it, but people find their own truth in the forms and colors of the thing itself. She was unique and questioning in a world that valued conformity and obedience of its women. Those who reported on her to Sandar measured her against a standard he cared nothing about. They would have made a good marriage. Quite possibly a noisy one, but a fine one.

He walked Zac through the streets of Jerusalem back to

the market where he had left Joseph and Mary. He found Mary standing quietly, Joseph gathering their belongings.

"I'm grateful for your thoughtfulness in acting that nothing is amiss," Sandar said. "My suit was not successful."

Joseph said, "You've been a champion for us; it's hardly possible to imagine that you would not succeed."

Sandar chuckled. "Robbers are no challenge compared to a strong woman."

"Your story is not over," Mary said.

Sandar had given up attempting to understand everything Mary and Joseph said, but he asked, "What? *My* story?"

She was looking over his shoulder. Sandar looked behind him. He saw only the crowds of the market, thinning now as close of day approached.

"What?"

"You were eloquent in your suit, no?"

"So I imagined in the event," Sandar said. "Perhaps not so, or too much so."

She continued to look past him into the crowded street.

She smiled. "And charming," she said.

He turned again to look, and again saw only the people beginning to return to their homes and some of the merchants preparing to cover and pack their wares.

Mary said, "I feel it to have been so. It could scarcely have been otherwise." She continued to look into the distance behind him.

Sandar looked again and this time, at the reach of his vision, he saw a figure bobbing above the crowd. Someone on a donkey, barely visible.

Now a woman came into view, a tall woman on a tall donkey, her head covered.

"Susannah!"

Sandar ran to her. "Susannah!" She looked down at him from her tall donkey. She was smiling. He opened his mouth to speak but no words came.

He led the pair to where Mary and Joseph were waiting.

"Our greetings, Susannah," Mary said.

"You're Mary," she said. "My greetings to you, and to Joseph as well. I know Sandar has told you of his business here in Jerusalem. I would be that business."

"Susannah," Sandar said. "What . . . ?"

"I was overcome," Susannah said. "A high emotion rose in me, a warmth and excitement came over me. It was a terror and a thrill to see you before me, so different than I had imagined, and so – so suitable.

"It wasn't my way to have those feelings. I fought it. I fought it like the devil had overtaken me and the only way I knew how to resist those feelings was to flee their source, you, the man who had dared speak to me of love, the only one ever of the men father presented. And I believed it. I believed your words because I knew you spoke truly about me. You came as a stranger and yet spoke to me as would a man who knew my true heart. I cried and I cried and when I caught my breath I knew that crying – that wasn't my way either. I had not cried since I was a little girl, certainly never over a suitor. Then I understood your words that our old ways aren't ways at all – they're barriers to new ways."

She slid from the donkey. "Sandar, called the Builder," she said. *That music again*, he thought. She took his hands in hers. "With Joseph and Mary and the admirable Zac as my witnesses, I say to you that I will be your betrothed, if you still desire me." She leaned toward him and he bent forward. She kissed him on the cheek.

Sandar rose from her kiss. "You honor and surprise me, Susannah," he said. "Yes, I'm as ardent in my suit here in the market as I was in the house of Nathan. I'm ready for our journey. To Bethlehem and beyond. I begin it with great joy."

"As do I," she said. "But now that I've mastered my senses I will tell you something."

"The first of many things, I'm sure," Sandar said. "But let's hear it."

Susannah said, "You know I'm known as a difficult woman among those of our city."

"I've acknowledged that I've so heard," Sandar said, "and that I found it a flavor of difficulty that will spice my meals most pleasurably."

Susannah laughed. "I just want you to know that I'm likely to remain stubborn and judgmental and become a spine in your ribs."

Sandar was delighted at her words and at the playful way she delivered them. "I've shaped the stones of Galilee," he said. "I'm quite certain those skills will avail me nothing against your will. But I'm grateful for the warning."

Sandar laughed, Susannah laughed, and Joseph and Mary joined in. Joseph glanced at Mary with mild alarm, but she said, "A little laughter will not cause Jes – will not hasten my time." Joseph smiled at her and she smiled back; he was not the only one in danger of misspeaking.

For the first time in Sandar's presence, Joseph and Mary exchanged a kiss.

Joseph said, "That's a fine donkey, long of leg."

Susannah said, "Father was pleased when I emerged from my room with my head covered and my hair plaited rather hastily, although you see that it has come loose since. Mother returned shortly after Sandar left and when she saw me, of course there were many tears, and, I must say, more from me. And from father; yes, he was joyful. He insisted on giving me his best donkey as a betrothal gift and for us to begin our journey with Joseph and Mary. She is called Hannah, but unless you have food it's pointless to call her."

"Welcome, Hannah," Mary said.

Sandar said, "I mentioned I was returning to the market."

"Yes," she said. "With your size you were not hard to find. You neglected to mention that benefit in our interview." She stood back and seemed to take stock of the scene she saw before her. "But now, let us see what we are about here."

Susannah turned to Mary. "Your time."

"Near," Mary said.

"Have you felt –"

"No," Mary said.

"A woman doesn't reach her twenty-seventh year in Jerusalem without learning midwifery," Susannah said. "I have assisted at many additions to Jerusalem's people. I'm accustomed to the difficulties. I thought perhaps it would be my destiny to attend the birth of the Jews in this city, but it appears Sandar had other ideas he has bewitched me into accepting. But I will attend you, and be honored so to do."

Even Mary seemed startled at the gift of Susannah's skills. "It must be. I am grateful." She looked at Joseph, who nodded.

Susannah asked Joseph to open their bags, and she inspected their belongings. "We do not have enough fresh blankets for the birth and the baby. Sandar . . . ."

"I'm on my way," Sandar said. "Surely there's a merchant here with what we need. Come with me to tell me what's required. We'll need to move quickly before the shops shut with the sunset."

Joseph opened his sack to find money but Sandar waved him off.

Mary and Joseph watched the couple move through the marketplace. They saw several people greet the tall fair Susannah and look after her when she and the tall fair Sandar passed, first with surprise, then with approval.

"I never doubted you," Joseph said to Mary. "I never doubted the dreams God gave me of what was to come. Now God has provided for needs we were not even aware of with Sandar and Susannah."

"And Zac," Mary said.

∽

Sandar and Susannah returned with additional blankets and clothing and food. Sandar had found a rich blanket he bought for himself, crimson with white trim, and he insisted that Susannah select something warm for herself.

Late afternoon was ripening into evening. Sandar had

not made the trip from Jerusalem to Bethlehem before, but the merchants had told him that the journey could be completed in several hours if the group moved along smartly.

"Clear tonight," one of the merchants told them. "The earth will give up its heat with the sunset; a cold night to journey. You're wise to buy my blankets. Yesterday's snow – not much, but what a surprise so late in the season! It will have melted some today but may freeze again, so I hope your donkeys are sure-footed."

"Very sure-footed," Susannah said.

"And a full moon," the merchant said. "A blessing for the traveler, but also for robbers."

"My *gladius* and *makhaira* will rattle in the dark and shine in the moonlight and convey an unmistakable message to the bandit looking for an easy thieving."

"Caesar's thief enough," the merchant said. "Let him tax the bandits. Godspeed."

As they made their way back to Mary and Joseph, Susannah asked Sandar about brigands on the road.

"I won't begin our journey with lies, even comforting lies," Sandar said. "You know that Mary and Joseph were attacked by robbers on the road from Jericho. But now Joseph is alert; I'll speak to him. And surely God would not countenance two attacks on these gentle people in a single day."

"And two not-so-gentle people," Susannah said. "I'll give up nothing quietly." Sandar chuckled. "You know that, do you not?" she said, as Sandar nodded. "Do you have extra weapons?"

Sandar was about to protest that he would not allow

Susannah to arm herself but thought better of giving any orders at this fledgling state of their betrothal. "Let me speak to Joseph and we'll see what we have between us."

Susannah laughed. "I sense that's no answer," she said. "I'll let it pass, since I myself have no experience in fighting off bandits, although I've had to brandish my walking staff at some forward young men at the market." Sandar had noticed the long stout cane secured to Hannah when Susannah had found their group in the market. In angry-enough hands it might provide a formidable defense.

"Mary objects to killing robbers," Sandar said.

"Does she now?" Susannah said. "Perhaps she and I can discuss the vagaries attending a fight with blades on the roadside at night."

When they returned to the market, they found Mary and Joseph standing and ready to depart.

"You're not to be standing," Susannah said to Mary. "We'll need a few minutes to arrange the packs on the donkeys, so please be relaxed where you were and we'll be ready shortly."

"I'll help," Mary said.

"That won't be necessary," Susannah said. "And besides, I have a special task for you."

"What task?"

"First, sit."

Mary promptly sat on the stone bench on which she had been resting.

"It's another miracle," Sandar whispered.

"There's nothing God can't do," Joseph replied.

Susannah said, "Please do me the honor of plaiting my

hair so that I may respect my betrothed with an appearance suitable to our status. I've never been very good at it."

"Your hair is fine and lovely and does not want to be told what to do, like the woman it adorns," Mary laughed. "But yes. Sit beside me and we will impose some dignity on it for our journey."

CHAPTER 12

The Road to Bethlehem

WHILE MARY QUICKLY created a firm braid out of Susannah's silky mane, Sandar and Joseph distributed all of the belongings and supplies across the rumps of the big donkeys. Sandar carried his large shoulder bag, and he had purchased one for Joseph to replace the worn handsack he had been carrying since Nazareth. Hannah got a new horsebag.

Mary rode Zac while Susannah rode beside her on Hannah. Joseph and Sandar walked ahead, their strides long and brisk to shorten the journey to Bethlehem. Sandar was relieved that Susannah would attend Mary should the rigors of this final leg of their journey bring Mary's time upon her before they found a place to spend the night's uncertain hours in the village.

Sandar sensed that Joseph would like to have spoken – it may have been a while since he had enjoyed the company of men. The eventful day left them alone with their thoughts as they walked south from Jerusalem accompanied by their lengthening shadows.

Sandar looked into the brush.

"What?" Joseph said.

"I thought I saw something," Sandar said. "It was nothing. A rabbit, nothing."

It was not nothing. But by the time he turned to face what he sensed, all he saw was the long tawny tail tipped with the black brush disappearing into the undergrowth. *He could not have followed us through Jerusalem*, Sandar thought.

Perhaps he had imagined it. Sandar was weary – he had been on the move and repeatedly challenged since before daybreak in Jericho – but he knew the day's journey would have an end in Bethlehem a few hours ahead. What end, he did not know. He shook off his tiredness and thought about what an extraordinary two days and nights it had been in his life, and resolved to remember it each year with Susannah as he recalled its drama and curiosities:

There were the sparkling, throbbing sky and stones and trees of the Judean desert.

There was the previous evening's encounter with Herod's searchers, the learned men of the stars, not even quite knowing what they were looking for. And their crazy story of the frog visitation of Jerusalem and how it brought them before one of the strongest, cruelest kings in the world.

There was the disturbing impression left by Ogen, captain of Herod's guard.

There was his coming upon the two poor travelers at the exact moment of the attack by the robbers, and his appropriation of their coins and jewels – what would he do with them? He thought of the orphan's home in Nazareth. And perhaps Susannah would know a needy cause in Jerusalem.

There was his new acquaintance with Mary and Joseph, a couple like no other he had ever known, convinced despite their low estate of some kind of grand secret destiny they demanded to live out.

There were Mary's quiet observations that hinted at some private knowledge, even foresight.

There was his unanswered question of why they were insisting that she give birth in Bethlehem.

There was the mysterious spying of the Lion.

There was the Fox returned to life.

There was his lively but failed encounter with Susannah at the house of Nathan.

And there was that same encounter turned unexpectedly successful with her reappearance and acceptance of him at the market, bringing with her the midwife skills of which their little company would soon have need.

And now, a moonlit trip to Bethlehem that would end – how? Bloodshed with robbers? A roadside birth in the cold? A comfortable lodging for them all? Some other startling event to go along with all the others of these days?

These dramas of his journey crowded out the melancholy of his recent months. *Perhaps I should travel more*, he thought; *engage more with the world beyond those who seek my services. Susannah would like that. Heh, I all but promised it to her.* He felt that perhaps there was meaning in the singular and wholly unforeseen course of the past day and evening. Some value being etched onto his life that was both within his grasp but beyond his senses, something mysterious but yet as concrete as putting one foot before another on the road to Bethlehem.

Perhaps I'm wrong that God does not act in the world in this age as He did in the scriptures' accounts from the hundred-years. Perhaps every – every thing that happens is His act. Of course, it is, but more, more! — perhaps every thing that happens is Him – Himself – and His meaning resides all around us if we will only perceive it truly and seek to know it without guile and love of self.

He was not sure how to do that. He was not even sure of the meaning of what he had just thought. He was not even sure it had a meaning.

The shadows of the day had disappeared. The moon was large and orange against the horizon in the east and would soon be making new ghostly shapes on the ground. He said to Joseph, "You mentioned you had packed some tools."

"I did," Joseph said. He told Sandar of the few items he had, things that were not too difficult to pack and carry. "And," he added, "they're sharp tools, if I understand your question."

"You do. I don't believe we'll have any trouble on the road," Sandar said. "Bethlehem is not so far from Jerusalem and Herod has started sending guards with the tax collectors. Robbers should be more wary. But it might be wise to have handy –"

Joseph smiled and produced an awl and a small ax from the folds of his tunic and the blanket that now covered him against the chill. "Perhaps we need not mention this to Mary," he said. "Her faith is strong, but I'm thinking we honor God by using the tools he suffers us to have invented to protect those of us who believe in Him against evil, just as we use them to build shelters to protect against the weather."

"A tool merely extends and refines the hand," Sandar said. "As we raise our hand in defense, so we may raise the mallet."

Joseph said, "I'd prefer that sword of yours unless I'm fighting a nail."

Sandar laughed. *Mary is not the only one of this union to speak wisely. The child will be fortunate indeed.*

The unexpected snowfall the merchant mentioned had disappeared except for thin patches that remained on either side of the road, and the surrounding hills displayed some glittering remnants. The sheep of the herds in this part of the country would have no trouble getting at the grasses beneath it. The spring's rains would take it away soon. Sandar was grateful for the clear night, although he thought about breaking out some of the blankets to warm the party as night fell and the earth returned the sun's heat to the firmament. The road itself was dry and safe.

Joseph wore only a thin coat over his tunic. He seemed to be thinking about something that shrugged off the weariness of their journey and the night's chill. Sandar considered that Joseph's and Mary's day had to have been at least as long as his, and he had spent some of his on Zac. But Joseph's step remained resolute and kept up with Sandar's longer stride without difficulty.

Sandar thought he knew the answer to this question, but he asked: "Do you or Mary have family in Bethlehem who might take you in? Mary's confinement is not likely to be lengthy."

"No," Joseph said. "Neither of us knows anyone there."

"Do you know of any lodging there?"

"No."

"You were right," Sandar said. "Your faith is strong indeed. I regret I don't have great familiarity with that village either. I would not expect more than one or two lodgings for hire, perhaps none, and the night will be well advanced."

Joseph said. "We knew we would encounter difficulties along the way for which we would likely have no ready answer. I know it's difficult to understand why we felt we had to make the journey now. Perhaps there will come a time, perhaps soon, when we may make ourselves understood. Everything that has happened to us today has strengthened Mary and me in our faith that God is watching over us."

Sandar stopped and held out his arm to stop Joseph. "I hope God is watching now," he said. He turned and ran back to Mary and Susannah on the donkeys and gestured for Joseph to join him. The donkeys halted on his arrival.

"Listen," he said.

The moon had been climbing but was far from the meridian. The shadows it cast remained long. The trees east of the road were plainly visible in the moonglow but the grove was dark within. The group heard the faint sound of snapping undergrowth and mumbling. Then, a sound that could only be frightening in exactly those circumstances – a donkey braying.

Sandar pulled his *gladius* slowly from its scabbard and made as much noise as possible. He held it high to catch the moon's light and rotated it slowly so that the flat of the blade might reflect into the grove. Susannah worked her walking staff out of its holder. Joseph felt into his garments for his awl and ax but did not bring them out. Mary sat quietly, no more perturbed than if Zac had slowed to sample some roadside grasses.

"Do not advance!" Sandar shouted. "We are poor travelers but we're rich in weapons and skill in using them. I will kill any man who shows himself. See me from your hiding place! See me as I stand in the moonlight! I have walked out of the Forum under the skyward thumb of Augustus himself and I promise you I will continue to walk this road tonight though my sandals may slip on your blood!"

The grove fell silent.

Then the footfalls and whispers grew louder and in the same moment, Susannah threw back her head and delivered an unearthly, ear-numbing howl.

'AAAIIEEEEEEEEEEEEEEEEEEEE, YI-YI-YI!! AHHHOOOOOOOO, YIP! YEEP-YEEP-YEEP-YEEP-YEEEEEEOOOWWWWWOOOOOOOOO!!"

And then, without a pause, she screamed, a full-throated

shriek of the sort that had defended women for millennia. She screamed until she ran out of breath, she gulped more air, and screamed again, and again.

Sandar and Joseph turned to stare at her.

Mary's features lit up with delight.

"THE FULL MOON CALLS ME!" Susannah shouted. "SPEAK, SING TO YOUR SERVANT! DIANE, JUNO, OLD SELENE OF THE GREEKS, GATHER TOGETHER IN ALL-SEEING LUNA AND GUARD THIS TRAIN FROM THE VIOLENCE OF THE UNBELIEVERS! JUDGE THEM AND SENTENCE THEM TO TASTE MY WRATH!

"I THANK YOU MY MOON, I PRAISE YOU FOR THE BLESSING OF THESE CLAWS AND FANGS AND I PRAY, I *PRAY* I SHALL HAVE THE CHANCE TO DRIVE THESE SONS OF SWINE BEFORE ME, TO RIP THEIR LAMENTATIONS FROM THEIR LYING THIEVING THROATS AND EXPOSE THEIR BOWELS TO THE WOLVES OF JUDEA!

"AAAIIEEEEE!! I WILL CIRCUMCISE THESE INFIDEL BEASTS WHETHER THEY REQUIRE IT OR NOT!"

Susannah slid from Hannah, who was showing signs of uneasiness at the racket issuing from the madwoman he was bearing. She whacked her walking staff three times on the hard pack of the roadway and now roared like a hungry pack of Jerusalem's stray mastiffs was coming alive in her.

When she stopped roaring and appeared to have regained herself, the group turned from her and stared into the looming grove. They heard movement but no voices, and whoever had gathered there seemed to be retreating deeper into the trees. After a few moments, the trees were silent again, save for the slightest of breezes.

"Let's keep moving," Sandar said, then he whispered to the group: "Say nothing of Susannah's actions. Don't look at her. Let her mount Hannah and we'll move ahead as though her fury and threats were an event to which we're accustomed."

Susannah nodded and got Hannah settled enough to remount. With her wrap, she dabbed at the sweat of her face that was already threatening to freeze in the night air.

Mary laughed softly and whispered, "Tonight, God puts the old dead foreign gods to good use," she said. "And even the Romans' disgraceful contests."

"I was not a gladiator," Sandar said.

"I know," Mary said. "You have been a mason and woodworker from your youth."

"I would have preferred not to lie," Sandar said, although he was not sure why he was apologizing for that. Something about Mary, and Joseph, too, and, in fact, the entire day made the world seem in charge and ready to judge but also to forgive in the cause of good sense and peace and kindness.

"So odd," Susannah said softly. "I repent my calling out to the foolish gods of the Romans and Greeks, and at the animal crazedness that I've never before displayed. The words and sounds seemed to come from outside of me."

Mary said, "We'll move past all that. The deity does not exist who did not hear you in your anger. The one God undoubtedly saw our trouble and heard the defense you sent to the sky, and heard your lie too, Sandar, and has already excused you both. And also Joseph for hiding tools in his clothing."

Joseph shook his head and smiled at Sandar. "It's always like this," he said.

"And He's forgiven me for the pleasure I took in your deceptions," Mary said.

Sandar said, "We ought not be too pleased with ourselves. This danger isn't over. In this moonlight they could see we're only four, with two women. They may only have retreated to reconsider their plan."

Sandar and Joseph walked ahead as they had been doing before the disturbance in the dark forest.

Joseph laughed softly. "Your betrothed," he said.

"My betrothed," Sandar sighed. "And yours."

"Both our lives promise great drama."

"I would have run, too, if I had heard that wailing," Sandar said. "I'm hopeful Susannah's rant does not reflect a strong opinion about circumcision."

"I sense Susannah has few weak opinions," Joseph said. "Do you think she was possessed?"

"No," Sandar said.

"Nor do I," Joseph said.

"Perhaps . . . inspired. Inspired by . . . something."

Joseph laughed. "That sounds like possession, although of a benign sort."

"This day," Sandar said, "This day."

"And this night," Joseph said.

Susannah had been keeping Zac close to Hannah. She reached out to steady Mary from time to time as she relaxed on this final leg of the journey. She felt Mary suddenly straighten.

"What is it?" Susannah said.

Mary had both hands on her belly.

"Your time?" Susannah said.

Mary shook her head. "I think it's not," she said. "I think he's excited that his birthplace is near. He'll calm in a moment."

Joseph had overheard and came running back to the two women, who had stopped. Sandar followed.

"You believe it's a boy?" Susannah said.

Joseph looked at her with alarm.

Mary waved off the question. "Oh, I don't know," she said. "I guess it's been so active, I just assumed. If it's a girl, God help the little boys of Nazareth."

"Every new mother guesses," Susannah said.

"Do they guess well?" Sandar said.

"No. Only right half the time. They might as well have drawn straws."

Sandar looked at Mary; he knew she knew. "We ignore Mary's third eye at our risk," he said.

Mary knew his thought and smiled her Mary-smile. "We always see others more clearly than ourselves, isn't that so?"

"So they say," Sandar said.

"Everything is fine," Susannah said. "He's just getting comfortable. Ha, now Mary's got me thinking boy. No need to stop."

Mary gave another little jerk. "I always think I've gotten used to the idea of this new life in me," she said, "then he kicks to remind me he's not just a dream, not just the s–. He's a person."

Sandar and Joseph had resumed their rapid march ahead of the women.

Sandar said, "Whatever your baby turns out to be, its instincts are good. I think Bethlehem is not far. It appears your wish that she be delivered there will come to pass."

"I'm certain of it, and all thanks to you for your faith in us" Joseph said. "Thanks also for Susannah. You can hear; I believe they have been speaking of the first days of care for the child and I'm sure it has taken her mind off of her condition. Still, with each hill I'm glad to think the moon will reveal buildings just beyond."

Sandar did not hear what Joseph said. He had begun to watch the sky.

He said to Joseph, "Don't move suddenly. After a bit, look at the sky as though you're doing nothing more than admiring the stars. More overhead than at the horizon. There are not many stars to see on a bright moonlight night, but pick a patch of sky and watch it for a few moments. Keep walking at our pace."

Joseph did as Sandar asked.

"Tell me what you see," Sandar said. "Keep your voice low."

"I – I cannot say," Joseph said.

"Do you see the dark shapes?"

"I see the stars wink out and then reappear as though – some things are moving across the sky that are not visible to us. Do you think they're clouds?"

"Moving too fast," Sandar said, "and in many different

directions. And you should be able to make out clouds on a moonlit night."

"What is it?" Joseph said. "Are you frightened?"

"I don't believe I am," Sandar said. "No, I'm not."

The moon disappeared, blacking the road and roadside for less than a second before it reappeared full and bright.

Susannah called out, "Did you see that?"

"Cloud," Sandar called back. "Must be windy above us."

He sensed skepticism from aboard Hannah behind him, but Susannah did not press the matter.

"It's like . . . ," Joseph said. "I don't . . . ."

"It's like something is gathering this side of the sky," Sandar said. "Perhaps I should be frightened, but I consider that despite the threats we've faced, no harm has come to us since I encountered you and Mary this morning. And good fortune has found me with my somewhat delayed betrothal to Susannah. I meant to ask you earlier . . . ."

"Yes?" Joseph said.

"On the road to Jerusalem . . . the sky, the roadside, rocks and trees. Especially the sky."

"Something there you thought you were seeing, even seeing clearly, but perhaps was not really there?" Joseph said. "But everything a little brighter, the lights and darks and colors more vivid and glittering, the plants more alive, the sky aswirl but completely cloudless, as though this were all at the edges of our vision, or perhaps imagined."

"Yes!" Sandar said. "You have put it perfectly! I thought perhaps my fatigue or the heat of the journey or not enough food or water before I set out, but you saw the same, or felt it."

"It was like the earth had been shaken awake," Joseph said.

"I felt it was telling me that something was about to change. Then I met the magi with their strange story about the frogs taking over Jerusalem. I'm thinking that nature wants us to start paying attention."

Joseph laughed. "I had myself considered whether to ask you if you had noticed it. When it was over I turned to Mary and – "

"She smiled."

"You have come to know her well," Joseph said.

"And then she said something where her meaning was . . . elusive?"

"Very well indeed, I should say."

"What did she say?"

"Nothing, at first. Then she looked around and up at the sky and said, 'God said to Moses, "I am."'"

"What did you say?" Sandar asked.

"'Yes,'" Joseph said, "'He is.'"

৵

A voice: "*Who* is?"

Before them stood the fat and skinny robbers. With them were several other robbers, including one enormous robber, heavy, but hard and tall. The enormous robber held a spear.

Sandar drew his *gladius*. Joseph brought out the awl and ax. Susannah jumped from Hannah and took her large walking stick from its holder.

The fat robber surveyed these defenses and laughed. He nodded, and the robbers unsheathed swords and daggers.

"Well, Sandar the Builder," the fat robber said. "Good evening. Perhaps I should thank you for taking such good care of my valuables. My friends and I can take them from here."

The travelers said nothing. Susannah and Joseph were brave, Sandar knew, and Mary was her usual impassive self, but if they resisted these odds would result in nothing but blood.

"You see, I've brought my own giant this time. But I'm not without some gratitude for you letting me and my partner" – he gestured to the skinny robber, who was trying to look fierce – "leave the scene intact this morning. Turn it all over without any foolish bravery, and I'll forgive your injury to my – I won't describe your schoolboy tactic in the presence of women. And I'll have your purse, Builder."

He leered at Susannah. "And that of your . . . interesting new companion."

Joseph spoke: "Sandar, we have no use for the coins and jewels."

There was not much to think over.

Sandar moved slowly to Zac, with Mary still aboard. She smiled her Mary-smile at him as he approached.

As he began to untie the straps holding the bags with the loot, he felt eyes on him. Zac had turned his head and was staring at him without blinking. Zac had never done that before; he paused and returned Zac's stare. Zac had never let him down, but under the donkey's gaze, Sandar felt as though he himself were threatening disloyalty to some unspoken expectation of his truehearted friend.

Sandar straightened from the packs. "No," he said.

"Corpses have no use for jewels and gold!" the fat robber said. "Quit stalling!"

Sandar looked from Zac to Mary. She looked at him with something akin to delight. Sandar hadn't forgotten the robbers' threat, but he returned her smile. "This is a day like no other," he said.

"Forget the bags!" the fat robber said. "We'll take the donkey –"

From behind the travelers came an animal scream.

The Fox was in the road. He raised his head and screamed again, and a third time.

"Shut your dog up!" the fat robber said.

"That is no dog," Susannah said.

The fat robber turned to the giant robber. "Shut that dog up!"

The giant robber stood forward and flung his spear at the Fox. It skittered sideways. The spear barely missed.

The Fox screamed again.

From somewhere in the brush, another fox screamed. Then another, further off. Another, even more distant. The next moment all the foxes were screaming.

"To the devil with all this racket!" the fat robber called. "Get them!"

Before the line of robbers took a single step, the Lion leapt into the road. He spun to one group, then to the other, snarling and roaring, as though celebrating his good fortune in encountering this bounty of flesh.

Joseph ran to Mary's side.

The Lion stopped his threatening dance. He faced the travelers and regarded Mary and Joseph with some care. He turned to Sandar and looked him over with equal thoroughness. Sandar was surprised that neither Zac nor Hannah was frightened of the Lion, who under other circumstances might have brought them to an efficient and nourishing end.

Having surveyed the travelers, the Lion spun to face the robbers. He snarled twice, then roared.

He walked toward the robbers. One of them fainted. The Lion sniffed at the man on the ground and grunted.

The Lion moved to the giant robber, who stood petrified. He noisily sniffed the big man, down and up. He made a sour face and sneezed, then released an earsplitting roar into the man's face. The giant robber spun and fled, as did half the robbers.

"Where are you going?" the fat robber screamed. "Fools! Lions won't attack a man! Hold your ground! Your fortune sits on the rump of that ass not twenty cubits from where you stand!"

"Moshe," the skinny robber said to his partner, reaching out to touch his tunic. "Moshe."

"We all have swords and they have one between them and a girl with a pole! I won't be robbed twice in one day! The lion hasn't touched any of us. I told you, *lions don't attack people.*"

The fat robber began to run towards Zac and the bags.

The Lion's feet didn't touch the ground as he launched himself. The fat robber was fat but the Lion's mouth opened wide and took him like a dog snatching a scrap of mutton tossed its way. The Lion shook the fat robber and dragged him screaming into the brush. As the fat robber's screams grew fainter and fainter, the remaining robbers ran the other direction. Except for the skinny robber, who stood transfixed.

The group looked up at Mary.

"I was misinformed," she said.

The skinny robber stood before the group, sword in hand. Sandar gave his *gladius* a shake; Susannah waved her pole threateningly.

The skinny robber looked about to cry. He said, "This has not been a good day."

No one moved.

"Do you have any more lions?"

He looked to Mary on Zac, Joseph alongside.

"Who *are* you?"

Sandar tapped his *gladius* on the ground. The skinny robber tossed his sword aside.

"I'm sorry . . . I'm – I'm sorry."

He looked to the ground and shook his head.

"I'm not good at this. I'm always running away . . . and my stomach hurts."

"What's your name?" Sandar said.

"Gidon," the skinny robber said.

Susannah snickered.

"I know," the skinny robber said. "'Mighty warrior.'"

The skinny robber backed away, then turned and started toward the brush opposite the Lion's exit. He stopped and looked back.

"Thank you." He walked away into the night.

The travelers turned together to look behind them. The Fox was gone.

CHAPTER 13

At the Inn

THE STREETS OF little Bethlehem were quiet. Its shadows were shrinking as the moon rose, and moonlight washed the city's walls and ways in a pallid blue.

They entered the town and wandered its streets for a short time before spotting a large building some little ways beyond the edge of town next to one of the hills to the east. Through the shutters they could see the flickering of lamps.

Across a broad alley from it – what was that, a stable?

When Joseph and Sandar entered the building they found a small tavern and a keeper's table. The room was littered with damaged lumber, the corpses of tables and chairs and benches. Beyond that was a passageway to what appeared to be a large room, although it was dark. The keeper, a short young man with unkempt hair and beard, heard them enter and came out to greet them.

"We're four," Joseph said. "Two women and the two of us."

The keeper held up his hand. "No room even for one with no woman," he said. "We have been filling up before sundown for the past several weeks."

"No room at all?" Sandar said.

"I try to accommodate as many travelers as I can," the keeper said. "My good nature got the better of me last evening, as there was not space enough in the great room behind me here for the blankets and pallets of the travelers I had admitted. Some men began to quarrel and a fight broke out that spilled out into this room. Some shepherds out here were drunk and joined the riot for no reason at all, and you can see the results." He gestured to the busted furniture. "I know the man who owns their sheep; perhaps he'll stand for replacing some of these items."

"I saw separate rooms at the back of the building and above," Joseph said.

"There are six," the keeper said. "An elderly man and wife. A wealthy man who is traveling with an armed soldier. A tax collector from Jerusalem and a room full of guards. A couple, the woman was very difficult. And a single traveler who did not speak Hebrew."

"Perhaps one of them would give up a room for gold," Sandar said.

"They have all retired," the keeper said, "and I won't disturb them. Besides, there is no other place for them to stay."

"The taxes," Sandar said, "and the census."

"Aye," the keeper said. "Taxes sweeten no one's mood. The city of David –" he spread his arms – "so many Jews wish to claim through him, so this where they must come to register and pay. Ach, I should not suggest that they claim falsely, no one would make the trip here unless they had to. With David's wives and concubines it's not surprising that his tree has so many branches. His lines could populate a city on their own. Perhaps you . . . ."

"Yes," Joseph said, "though his son Solomon."

"Ah," the keeper said, "with Bathsheba. That's a fine son through which to find David, the best, a king! But I'm sorry to say it does not enlarge my inn for your party."

"I mentioned gold," Sandar said. "Might there be room in your own lodging for one night? We would be quiet and cause no trouble." He and Joseph shared a quick glance, each considering whether the birth of a child could fairly be characterized as trouble-free quiet.

He gestured with his head to the great dark room down the hall behind him. "One of those pallets is mine," he said. "My father owns this inn. My brother operates the stable."

"And your father . . . ," said Sandar.

"Lives in Jerusalem," the keeper said.

"Your brother . . . ."

"Has a pallet of his own," the keeper said.

"This room," Joseph said. "We could make room."

The keeper said, "I like gold as much as the next man, perhaps a little more, may God forgive me. But I'll be rising in a few hours to clear out this mess and scrub the wine and blood from the floor. And it's the only way in and out for travelers, some of whom I expect to depart before sunrise. I'm thinking that your women need privacy."

"They do," Sandar said. "Are there other inns?"

The keeper said there were none.

During the journey with Mary and Joseph, Sandar had tried to put out of his mind the certainty that this was what they would face in Bethlehem. Ever since he had encountered the couple, he felt control of his own life slipping away as he gradually talked himself into doing something that made no sense and for which the couple had offered no explanation. Even as the miracles of these days and nights cleared the path for their journey, he felt like he was gradually shrugging off his reputation as a hard-nosed businessman of Nazareth to indulge the foolishness of what were little more than a boy and a girl who found their circumstances as boys and girls sometimes do. Although they did not seem foolish; they did not speak foolishly, and they pursued their intention with thorough seriousness. Perhaps their luck had just run out in Bethlehem.

Joseph said, "Thank you, sir. We understand your situation."

"It's nothing," the keeper said. "I'm frequently awakened by night travelers. I regret my imagination is not suggesting an answer for your party on this cold night. May God protect you and your women."

As they left the inn, they heard Susannah calling softly to them from the entrance to the stable across the alley. "Mary and I have found our lodging for the night," she said. "Follow."

She walked Sandar and Joseph down the alley that ran between the inn and the stable. The far end of the path opened into a broad, shallow cave in the side of the hill next to the inn. Mary was half-sitting on the edge of a long stone manger outside the cave mouth, holding her belly. A ragged donkey and an old ram jostled each other searching for some stray grain at the manger's far end.

"We can sleep here, and deliver the baby if it decides to appear," Susannah said.

"It will do," Mary said. "As I have considered it with Susannah, I believe it's ideal for what is to come."

Sandar was prepared to object, but he noticed that Joseph was already unpacking some of the blankets and other supplies. Susannah had found a palm frond and was sweeping the floor of the cave.

"This is exactly the right place," Joseph said to Sandar. "You'll see."

"At least let me check the structure," Sandar said, although, apparently like Joseph who continued his preparation to make the cave their accommodation for the night, he had determined that there was little to gain in disputing with either of these women no matter what he found. And he had no better answer. Still, he was a builder, and he had women and a new generation in his charge, and he was going to exercise the care his instincts demanded.

Why is this here? he thought. *Someone must have really wanted to put a cave here to carve it out of solid rock.* Unlike the stable, at least it had a roof. But it was so shallow that it provided little protection from the weather. Or Sandar thought, from anything.

And yet – here it was.

He made Mary leave the cave while he tested the walls and the ceiling. He climbed onto the hillside to ensure that the rock above the cave was stable and free from faults, at least as much as he could discern in the light of the moon. Inside, some cracks and gaps had been mortared over, but quite competently. Sandar poked at the ceiling with a branch he found, but no crumbs fell. He saw no dust or pebbles in the stone manger that might have fallen from the structure.

"It will do," he said. "For tonight."

Susannah bade him join her outside the cave along the stable path. "Did you see that manger at the cave?" she whispered. "Mary wants to place the baby in it if it comes tonight."

"Our circumstances do require some improvisation in furnishing a nursery," Sandar said.

They heard Mary's faint voice. "He – it will come tonight."

Susannah said, "How did she know – hear . . . ?"

Sandar shook his head. "The day . . . her words, her understanding . . . I don't know. You begin to understand why I felt drawn to her and Joseph. And, I suppose, their baby."

"There is straw and grain scattered in the manger," she said. "And whatever the animals themselves have left there from their mouths as they feed. And it must be six, seven cubits long, that's no comfort for a child! No matter how many blankets you surround it with! Filthy, and entirely unsuitable for an infant! And the animals may well visit and nose around to see what is there for them." She made a face.

"And Sandar," she said.

"Yes, my Susannah?"

"The manger is *stone*. It's *stone*. Stone is *cold*. It's already cold, and the night is not yet as cold as it's going to get. We cannot lay the baby on *cold stone*, even wrapped in blankets."

Sandar was touched by Susannah's concern for the child's welfare and comfort. He thought briefly a man's thought that a newborn is not going to know to compare cold stone with other materials upon which it might have been placed to lay its head in its first hour of life. He savored instead the thought of Susannah focusing her care on her – their – own child someday.

"No, my Susannah," he said. "You're right. That would not be suitable for Mary's baby."

"Well?" she said. Sandar liked it that she thought he might have an instant solution for all of her concerns. He hoped to, always. "Why are you smiling?"

The circumstances of the day spoke to him.

"Another miracle awaits to solve this problem of the unsuitable manger." He took his purse from Zac and counted out a number of gold pieces. "Joseph, let's go visit the keeper and conclude our arrangements," he said. "I don't require your purse, but we'll need your strong back."

Sandar and Joseph reentered the front room of the inn. Sandar made just enough noise to alert the keeper without rousing the group bedded down in the large room beyond.

"Again, you visit me," the keeper said, shaking his shaggy head to chase the slumber. "No one has departed our rooms since your last visit, much less travelers who could be replaced by your party with two women." He spoke irritatedly at having to report the obvious.

"Is your brother here?" Sandar said. "The one who minds the stable? We return with a proposal that we believe he will find profitable."

"He's visiting my father in Jerusalem," the keeper said. "I mind the stable in his absence."

"Excellent," Sandar said. "Then we'll present our proposal to you."

"I'm sympathetic to your needs on this cold night with two women, but no proposal will create room out of no room," the keeper said. "I saw you have two donkeys. You may stable them here tonight. The stable is crowded but you can find an odd space if you look a bit. I'll require no payment, although I'm unsure of how much straw my brother left for travelers. I expect him late tomorrow."

Sandar said, "Our donkeys are grateful, but I mentioned profit."

The keeper showed skeptical interest.

"We'll worry about tomorrow's requirements tomorrow," Sandar said. "But tonight, our group would like to make our camp in that shallow cave adjoining the stable. We have enough blankets to keep us warm until morning and the hillside provides some protection. We would like perhaps six or seven lamps and oil as we may need light beyond what the moon can offer and they will give off some warmth.

"I've guessed at your charge for our party were we to have taken one of your separate rooms, and considered the value to use your lamps and oil and stable for the night. I've tripled that total and brought it in gold." Sandar quietly poured the coins from his pouch into his hand and placed them on the table in front of the keeper.

"I told you I'm like other men in desiring gold," the keeper said, "but this is too much, especially for an open cave on a cold night. I value my reputation among travelers in Judea and cannot accept –"

"I'm grateful to deal with a fair man who values the opinion of his customers," Sandar said. "But there is one more thing we request." He gestured to the room. "My friend and I are carpenters. We have need of some furniture, places for our women to sit. We'll take some of these scraps and fashion them to suit our requirements. We're skilled and can select pieces that will let us put them together quietly so your guests are not disturbed. When we depart, we'll leave them behind for you. Will you take my gold for our needs of this night?"

The keeper said, "I'm happy to let you take the scraps you need back to the cave and put them to use, and I can give you lamps and oil enough for the night." He was glad he was not going to have to remove all of the broken lumber in the room himself. He looked at the coins and separated them into two piles. He scooped the smaller pile into his palm. "This will be sufficient, perhaps more than sufficient, may God forgive me. I'll find some lamps and oil."

Sandar envisioned the baby's bed as a tiny manger. The two men conferred on the pieces needed and began sorting through the keeper's rubble. They salvaged nails that were not too badly bent from the evening's melee. He assigned Joseph the task of building a small open box that would be softened with straw on which to rest the child wrapped in blankets. Sandar would create a pair of crosslegs to elevate the miniature bed. The new crib would be rough, but stable enough, and warmer and more secure than the stone manger.

And, Sandar thought, it would make Susannah happy.

They gathered the lumber they needed for the new little manger, and claimed a couple of the damaged chairs to repair for Mary and Susannah. Sandar sent Joseph back to the stable to get started while he quietly dug through the rubble looking for one additional piece, something fine-grained, something that would take the knife without splitting. He found a healthy chunk that pleased him.

The men worked quickly. Where possible they fastened the damaged boards and members by fitted joints; where the wood was too poor or misshapen they used the nails, taking care to work as quietly as possible.

"It's rough," Sandar said to Susannah. "It rocks a bit on the uneven floor of this cave, and the legs themselves – we had no way to measure and we were working with trash. Joseph did fine work with what we were able to salvage."

Susannah held up a finger. "Hush," she said. She looked at the tiny wooden manger and ran her finger along one of the bedwalls. "A manger that rocks a bit is not such a bad thing." She rocked it slowly a couple of times.

"Your promise of a life of new ways has come true within hours," she said. "My betrothed. My betrothed. I'm fortunate indeed for father's command that I present myself to you. The little manger is beautiful for the needs of this night."

"I'm unsure who was presented to whom," Sandar said, "but I too consider myself possessed of the best fortune this day." He added, "My betrothed."

They slowly leaned toward one another and kissed, briefly and softly, like the new couple they were.

Susannah returned to Mary. She was sitting on one of the chairs from the inn Joseph had repaired. Susannah leaned down and spoke quietly to her. Mary smiled her Mary-smile and said, "Thanks be to you both. It will be a perfect bed for him."

Susannah wondered again at Mary's confidence in the baby's gender, and at her calm, as her time was surely soon.

CHAPTER 14

Waiting

SANDAR WALKED INTO the hills behind the cave and found a place to sit facing the still-rising moon. He took the piece of wood he had wrapped in a blanket and examined it with care, considering how it could best take the chisel and knife.

He had not shaved since the night before he left Nazareth. His stubble glinted white in the cold glow of the moon.

He held the chunk of waste wood from the tavern at arm's-length and turned it in the moonlight.

He smiled when he saw how to give it life.

Sandar stood in the moonlight on the scrubby hillside. He thought back to the moment he saw the robbers run from behind the rock to attack Mary and Joseph. Between that moment and this one he had not traveled far on the map, but in those miles and those hours his life – what? Yes, his course had changed dramatically with his betrothal to Susannah. But something else was happening, something even more than the advent of a new life in the cave by the stable.

He felt himself reaching into the night with an open hand. If there was anything out there it was beyond his reach. Yet also close, in the teasing song of the land and the sky and the riddlesome young couple he had befriended and felt bound to protect.

Sandar stared at the moon until it appeared to pulse in a breathing sky.

Susannah's voice: "What are you doing out here?"

"Thinking about the morning," Sandar said, slightly regretting the slight lie. "It will come eventually."

"Much may happen between now and then," Susannah said. "I think it's likely."

"Mary . . . ."

"Resting. She's quiet but she seems almost joyful. She allowed me to examine her – not intimately, but just to feel her belly and how she is carrying. It's hard even for a physician to tell, but I've been called to be with many young women waiting for their firstborn and it's just a feeling I get. I believe the baby will come within hours. Mary herself believes this, as you heard."

"She's so young," Sandar said.

"Very young and strong," Susannah said, "But from the way she has moved this afternoon and evening and from what I observed when I examined her, small as she is she has a good form for childbirth and the child is well-placed in the womb. But one never knows until the event."

"Joseph?"

Susannah rolled her eyes. "The sweet man. As the time grows near he's about to jump into the sky with nerves. I've tried to comfort him. I sent him to get clean water from the well we passed on the way in but he must have run because he was back almost before I could return to Mary. I felt that he would like to tell me something, but Mary nearby seems to quiet his tongue. I thought to keep him away from her in his state, but when he insisted on going to comfort her, it happened the other way around – she calmed him with only a few words and her hand on his."

"I'll return with you to keep Joseph company and wait for what we're waiting for. I'm sorry if I worried you."

Susannah said, "I wasn't worried. You defeated robbers three times and me once today. I didn't imagine that the hillside would hold much danger for you."

"I hope you didn't think of our coming together as a defeat."

Susannah stroked the blanket he had thrown over his shoulders. "No," she said. "We'll have to grow accustomed to one another's teasing."

Sandar liked the sound of that, *one another's teasing*. Perhaps he did not need to watch his speech around her as much as he had thought to do.

"Besides," Sandar said, "tonight's bandits in the woods seemed far more frightened of you than of me. And that last encounter – that was all the Fox and the Lion. And Zac, too, who shamed me into having faith in the magic of my last two days with those big brown donkey eyes of his."

"Magic – yes," she said. "My own reaction was – it was

like it was not my own reaction. When I heard the sounds in the woods, I found I wasn't fearful. I was angry not for myself – nor, may God forgive me, for you, my betrothed – but with the thought that poor Mary and Joseph were threatened again for what little they have and with all they had overcome to be on that road this night."

"And you acted," Sandar said.

"Without thinking. The words and the sounds and the feeling – I would never have imagined myself capable of it and in fact, it was like it was not me. It was not me."

Yes, Sandar thought, *much like my fine words for you when we met in the house of Nathan. Like my exhortation to Mary and Joseph when I learned their story on the road from Jericho.*

Sandar said, "Let's return to our friends and see what other surprises the night may hold."

﹆

Sandar bade Joseph walk with him on the streets near the stable. The little town was quiet and there was no breeze to cover the sound of their footsteps. The snow had mostly melted, leaving some puddles and mud that shone a warning in the moonlight. The skyshapes the men had noticed on the road to Bethlehem had vanished, or perhaps arrived at where they were going.

Sandar guided them some distance from the stable, until Joseph became nervous; he selected a winding route back to give the women as much time alone as possible. He wanted to occupy Joseph with man-talk of one subject or another, but Sandar had to admit that he himself would be happy to be elsewhere when Mary gave birth.

"You and Mary have endured much to be here this night," Sandar said.

"No more than you," Joseph said.

"You must feel relief that Mary's time is at hand."

"Yes," Joseph said. "Many questions will be answered."

While Sandar had grown accustomed to a certain coyness in Mary's and Joseph's speech, he had not stopped wondering at it.

"Your questions?" Sandar said.

Joseph did not respond.

Sandar said, "I hope to be a father someday."

Joseph walked with his thoughts.

He said, "I know Susannah told you to keep me out of their hair. I'm sorry that I'm not good company."

"Joseph," Sandar said, "you're an interesting man. There is strength in you but something within, something that's waiting to burst out and be declared to the world. You fight to keep something hidden."

"I'm a carpenter. My words are few and simple. They're unsuited to . . . certain things."

"What things?"

"If I could answer that question my words would be suited to them."

Sandar laughed. "So they would."

"You said that you dream," Joseph said.

"Yes, and not only in sleep."

"What do your dreams teach you?"

"This journey is teaching me I don't know what I thought I knew."

"No one can," Joseph said.

"What do you mean?

"Nothing. I don't know. It doesn't matter."

"But it does matter, doesn't it," Sandar said, "what we know of the world?"

Joseph stopped and faced Sandar.

"Yes!" he whispered as loudly as he dared. *"But the world changes tonight! Everything – changes – tonight!"*

Joseph looked back towards the stable. "I know I'm in the way, but I must be back to Mary."

Joseph turned and ran back to the cave. Sandar let him go. He had no response to Joseph's cryptic conclusion, nor any other strategy to keep him out of the women's way. He hoped that he and Joseph had not caused too much commotion in the quiet little village in the middle of the night.

It occurred to him that he had not tended to Zac and Hannah, and he made a detour to the well at Bethlehem's gate to see if the town left buckets there for travelers so he might take fresh water to them. Finding no containers at the well, he walked back.

Susannah was waiting for him in the alley next to the stable. The sleeves of her robe were wet and pink. Her eyes were glistening.

CHAPTER 15

It Begins

"THE CHILD!" SANDAR said. "It's come!"

"It is," Susannah said. "A boy. Mary was right."

"Of course!" Sandar laughed. "Were there troubles? I heard nothing."

"No. No."

"Mary is well?" Sandar said. "I hear a strain in your voice among your unusually few words."

"She is well," Susannah said. "She's resting. The birth was . . . remarkable."

"I must go to greet the newcomer," Sandar said.

"You may, but wait." Susannah touched the arm of his robe for him to stay and listen.

"I know you've seen many births," Sandar said, "so I wouldn't presume to read your thoughts on this one. But you seem troubled."

"Troubled, no," Susannah said. "But I'm wondering at what I've seen."

"Is this a happy wondering, or a puzzled one?" Sandar said.

"Truly, I don't know. My life with you begins with perplexity, but, I'm believing, great joy. It's possible you undersold what to expect in our journey."

Sandar said, "I'm accustomed to you speaking with directness, but now I'm reaching for your meaning."

"The birth," she said. "It was quick and very clean. Mary lost her water and her labor began right away. Mary is a small woman and the baby is big. She pushed bravely, but I had to pull like a galley slave to drag that boy into the world."

Susannah looked back towards the cave. "Some young women giving birth for the first time, it takes hours, and they suffer so! Mary fought hardly at all and did not call out. We used few of the blankets. I cut several of them up so we may keep the baby clean."

"But you've surely encountered the quick birth, the clean one, even the quiet one?" Sandar said.

"Yes, but it was still unusual, very – very unusual," Susannah said. "The boy is well-formed and alert – I've never seen a newborn follow another with his eyes like this one, and his coordination is almost frightening – but he didn't cry. Babies always cry when their breath comes and at first I thought maybe something was wrong, but no. He's big and healthy and active and drew air right away and was hungry for Mary. He was immediately ready to suckle and Mary had milk and fed him but only briefly until he was satisfied and ready to sleep. I wrapped him and we made a soft bed for him on the hay in the little manger you built. He's sleeping there now."

Sandar shook his head, as if to clear it for whatever Susannah seemed to be preparing to tell him, and searched her eyes.

They could hear Mary and Joseph talking in the cave, Joseph excited, Mary calm.

Susannah said, "Even though this is her first child Mary is an instinctive and willing mother. She showed great emotion, a great quiet joyfulness after I cleaned him and handed him to her to hold and feed. Finally, finally she is letting herself be tired after this long and difficult day and this most difficult thing a woman can do. Perhaps we can persuade Joseph to let her sleep."

"This all sounds wonderful, cause for delight," Sandar said. "She has delivered in Bethlehem as she and Joseph wished, and the birth was free from difficulty, or as free as it's possible for such a hard thing to be."

"I'm not learned in the arts of the physician," Susannah said, "nor familiar with all of the mysteries of our bodies, not even my own."

"What are you saying?" Sandar said. "Midwives are much honored for their wisdom and skill, don't be modest. What are you trying to say to me, or trying not to say?"

"Sandar," Susannah said.

Her voice dropped nearly to a whisper: "Mary is a maiden."

Sandar said nothing. His expression did not change.

"Mary is a maiden!" she whispered with additional heat. "A virgin!"

Sandar remained silent, as do men when confronted with the mysteries of women.

"I know it as I know my own hand!" she said. "It's a miracle. A miracle! A miracle I would have scoffed at had I heard it from another."

Sandar felt weak. He leaned against a wall.

"You have not sought the hand of a crazywoman," she said. "I saw what I saw. When I looked up at Mary –"

"She smiled her smile," Sandar said.

"Yes!" Susannah said. "Through all the pain, with all the blood, in the misery of that cave with the stink of the stock in her nostrils, she smiled!"

Sandar's mind boiled and churned as the truth ignited his heart.

"The young magician. And Joseph. They both tried to tell me."

"What?"

"A maiden. In Bethlehem . . . the miracles. It all . . . . Have you spoken to Joseph of this?"

"Ha! What under heaven would I have said to him? 'Congratulations, you're not a father'?" Susannah calmed. "He came into the cave and went immediately to Mary and the baby as soon as he was born," she said. "There was joy in his face but he held his words. I didn't speak to him other than to tell him it was a boychild and sound of body and that Mary was well, and he thanked me and asked God's blessings on me. I didn't know what to say to him."

Sandar felt a joy the silent night could barely contain.

"They have both known. Susannah! Something beyond our understanding, something, something beyond wonderful, has happened this night! This night, and this day, and in the belly of that maiden of Nazareth!"

Susannah said, "They have named him Jesus."

"'One who saves,'" Sandar said.

One of the prophets said his name would be Immanuel, "God with us." The same. He's . . . .

Sandar's head filled with what he had felt in the scrub hills west of Jericho, and in the sky, and in the words of the priests in the synagogue, and the astrologers at the tavern the night before. And the serenity and secret wisdom of the betrothed pair he met on the road to Jerusalem, and all that had happened to them and to him and now to Susannah, and he knew what he would find in the manger.

CHAPTER 16
Sandar's Dawn

JOSEPH ATTENDED MARY in the light of the oil lamps the keeper had provided. Their faces were full of the satisfaction that is felt when the expected has been accomplished. The baby was asleep in the little manger Sandar and Joseph had cobbled together an hour earlier, but Sandar's eyes remained on Mary and Joseph.

Mary said, "It's true, what Susannah has told you."

Sandar was no longer surprised at what Mary knew or said. And he himself knew it was true.

"It's as you have been taught," Joseph said. "As we all have been taught."

"Taught and foretold by the prophets of the hundred-years," Sandar said.

Joseph nodded. "You remember your lessons."

"The king of the Jews," Sandar said.

He fell to his knees next to the manger and looked

down at the child. He swiped the cap off his head and clasped it in his hands before him.

Jesus opened his eyes and looked at Sandar.

It was a newborn's face. He moved like a newborn. His small noises were those of a newborn. His thick black curls were wet. But his eyes found Sandar's and held them, as Susannah had told him.

Susannah had wrapped him in blankets but he had worked his arms free and was waving them about. She knelt beside him and reached in to resecure the swaddle.

Sandar said, "Wait."

He pulled his hillside work from a pouch he had secured to his belt.

"It's Zac!" Joseph said. "Look, he has even carved the notch in his left ear! And the flanks and chest, like a bull ox! It's Zac for sure."

"A poor gift for a king," Sandar said.

"It's beautiful," Mary said. "We'll treasure it always and tell him the story of brave Zac and the robbers, and that he carried me to Bethlehem so that he might be born as was foretold."

He placed the little wooden donkey on Jesus's belly.

Sandar thought a tiny smile had appeared on Jesus's face. His arm-waving stopped. He gripped one of the toy's legs.

Susannah said, "Splinters, Sandar, please! His skin is like silk. He joined us in this world less than a half-hour ago. I need to rewrap him or his little arms will freeze."

Without his fine carving tools, Sandar had done his best to cut and shape the wood, and smooth it with an oiled cloth and fine sand from the hillside. But for all his improvisation, his gift was little more than old unfinished wood in a donkey shape.

"Susannah's right; the toy is too rough," he said.

When Sandar pried the toy Zac from Jesus's infant grip, the boy grabbed his finger.

Sandar was shot through with an indescribable exhilaration, a lightning cavalcade of emotions, and even a drizzle of fear. Jesus's grasp was not the reflexive grip of the newborn – he sensed without doubt that Jesus's hold on his finger was born of intention, that the child was making a connection that he could not yet speak.

Jesus looked at Sandar with those strangely knowing eyes, not the unfocused squint of a newborn's always on the verge of sleep, but eyes fully open and taking in the world. Taking in the world, but also speaking to it from some bottomless pool of –

"Love!" Susannah said. "Look! So sweet."

Mary and Joseph were quiet.

Sandar whispered: "My king."

What is this? Sandar thought. *The child, he is sparkling, almost hidden behind a luminous mist.* He looked up at Susannah and at that moment felt beginning to spill from his eyes the brimmed tears that had captured the light from the flickering lamps.

The events of the day before and this day and this night pressed down on him and demanded that he speak their meaning. "The foretold king of the Jews, he is here before me as a child and I bring him a piece of wood shaped like an ass!"

"My betrothed," Susannah said, her own tears gathering. "You're not of the blood, you need not weep so or scorn your gift."

Sandar could not speak. He, the man who loomed over everyone he encountered, coughed great sobs he first tried to suppress; but as that was an old way, he released them as he knelt by the manger. His tears fell on the cap grasped in his folded hands. His head was bent low over the rough little bed and its serene new life.

His thoughts raced, tripped, tumbled over themselves in a fever of roiling wonder and instinctive certainty:

There is nothing for me but to weep and cry out!

These are tears of joy, tears of – of release!

This is Jesus! It is he!

This is what Mary and Joseph have known but withheld from me, fearful of the scorn of the day-to-day.

Jesus! 'One who saves.'

But saved from what? From what do I, Sandar the Builder, healthy and secure, require saving from a king of the Jews?

Sandar paused in his thoughts. Something was amiss, incomplete.

Susannah was right. Listening to the priests in the synagogue, even honoring the Jewish parents who took me in, none of it makes me a Jew. My blood is filled with the gods of my Greek and Roman ancestors and who knows what from the northlands. I'm marked by my foreskin as no Jew.

So — not my king.

Yet here I weep and can scarcely find breath at the edge of this rough bed.

He looked up from the manger but his brimming mind had no room for images and he saw nothing.

And yet I have led them. It is as Mary and Joseph have said:

I, Sandar the Builder and Nazarene and true Gentile, have been of their journey, their story, as I met the searching magi, drove off the bandits, protected and fed them on the way, brought them Susannah who defeated the danger in the woods and who was Jesus's first human touch at his birth of Mary, treated with the innkeeper, built the bed for his sweet head, and now guard the new family from the darkness.

Then, and even now —

He looked down at Jesus, his eyes filling again. He said: "You're right, Susannah. I'm not of the blood. I'm Gentile of the blood. But Mary said it:

"*I am of this story.*"

Sandar raised his head to Mary and Joseph.

"Not just king of the Jews." He spoke the words quietly.

"King of us all," Sandar said, "king of us all!"

Susannah touched his shoulder and said *hush* and Sandar caught himself and was quiet again.

"King of the new ways," he whispered as he turned again to the manger.

But he could not stay silent.

"You were wise to keep your peace, Joseph. And Mary, right to demand Bethlehem tonight. No ear of man could have been prepared to hear your dreams."

He became aware that Susannah was struggling with all that had happened, and now with Sandar's emotional reaction that was so unlike him. Or was it? She had known him for only hours.

He stood from the manger to face her. The words came and would not stop:

"It had to be this way.

"The new king had to be a newborn.

"Of common birth.

"In the most difficult, the most deprived of circumstances.

"He could not appear before us as a god or a king, or in Jerusalem or Rome as a conquering savior.

"He had to arrive as a helpless human. As a new human."

Sandar smiled at the bed made of scrap wood salvaged from the wreckage of fighting drunks.

"Susannah, see that despite his helplessness he is less bound to the world, less in thrall to its grip, than any of us!

"Because . . . because . . .

"He had to come to us from nothing.

"Free of the past.

"Free of alliances.

"Free of the jealousies and disputes and even pleasures of a palace.

"Free of the old ways, the old philosophies, the old teachings, even free of the demands and judgments of families, and even the rules of the temples.

"Pure and clean and untouched."

He looked at Mary.

"Free even of the touch of man."

Sandar had begun to breathe heavily but as understanding had come upon him he was calming.

So, so, so. This tiny one is not sent to save the Jews from want or from pain or from the oppression of Herod and Augustus and those following who would put on their wreaths of laurel and gold.

His tears had dried. He looked again at Mary and Joseph, who were beaming with joy and nodding at his understanding.

"He is free!" Sandar said. He began to laugh as he continued to gaze down into eyes of the life in the manger.

God and man, both but neither; a life entirely new.

Susannah's alarm at the passion of Sandar's speech was

starting to ebb as her understanding grew. But: "What have these things to do with a messiah to deliver the Jews from bondage?"

Sandar understood her question.

"Kings and armies have no corner on bondage, Susannah. It's not kings, it's the world from which we must be saved! Our world that hides all meaning from us, that is the disease from which we all suffer, and this perfect little king is sent of God to save us, to raise us up from this world to which we're bound, two feet on the earth, every day of our lives, closer to hell below than to the firmament of heaven. We're born we live, we work, we take our pleasure, we raise children, we die, after all that we die, and for what? The priests and teachers have no answer for that!"

Susannah bent to Jesus. "This isn't about Herod, or Rome."

"You feel it too, Susannah! It brought you to the marketplace today when you felt the truth of my promise that we would search for the new way, the way to throw off those bonds!"

"But he is only a baby."

"I felt it when he held my finger, when he looked at me," Sandar said.

"A Jew does not suffer the bonds of the world any more than does the Roman or the Greek or the Northman or the Egyptian or anyone! We're all trapped between

birth and death on this earth. And that prison is
sounder than any king could build!

"We must be as he is.

"We must be reborn in the world.

"We will raise him, and he will raise us up."

Sandar turned back to the manger. Jesus had taken advantage of Susannah's distraction to wiggle more thoroughly out of his wrapping. He was now waving both his arms and one free leg in seeming approval.

"And we have done nothing to deserve freedom, honoring God with useless words but not with our deeds, or our hearts. Jesus is a gift. A gift this night to all the nations."

"My betrothed," Susannah said, "your words are lovely – lovely and inspired. But we can't live at the command of poetry! How can the world change through a child who cannot even speak, much less lead?"

"The prophets themselves didn't know that! Yet here he lies as foretold! It's so, my fine words are only words and perhaps not even mine! Ha! All I know, *all* I know is that *this – this is how it must begin: from nothing*!"

"Tonight, I can only do what I can do," Susannah said. "He is born, so we must let him begin his life as an infant. He needs quiet, Mary needs calm – Joseph too – and this little one needs me to rewrap his bedclothes against this cold night. And we don't want to raise the inn at this hour. There will be time to talk about what has happened here."

She picked Jesus up gently from the manger and tucked his arms back in the wrap. "You're a strong one," she said, "and you're going to get an extra turn and an extra tuck to keep those sweet arms warm."

"Please bring him to me," Mary said.

Susannah bent to Mary with Jesus. Mary held him on her forearm and began to rock. In these few tender moments it seemed to Sandar that with Jesus's birth, the great task that had been thrust upon Mary and that had imbued her manner with such certainty and wisdom was accomplished, and she was again become the simple young girl of Nazareth, now a new mother like any other. "I want to look at him," she said. "I want to hold him as long as I can before . . . ." She shook her head, her words failing. Joseph straightened the blanket around her shoulders. "Before . . ."

Sandar stood. "Before the world comes for him," he said. "Before he makes himself known."

Joseph said, "We know only what he is this night, not what he is to become, or how, or when. We only know we must protect and raise him as God gives us the strength and the wisdom and the light."

"We won't resolve these things tonight," Susannah said. "Let us – let us . . . ." She caught her breath, about to weep again.

"Let us be free tonight in this glorious cave and fragrant stable," Sandar said, laughing.

He put his arm around Susannah, who was wiping the last of her tears.

He said:

"Let us awaken to this gift of the new morning."

❧

The oil lamps of the cave gave off little heat, but Sandar found that the excitement of his encounter with Jesus in the cave had warmed him. He walked into the alley to cool, and as he did, he wondered:

Why this cave? Of all the simple and even mean places to which God could have directed us, why was Jesus born out of doors?

Upon thinking that thought, it occurred to Sandar that on a journey where, it seemed, God had provided, perhaps the question was a bit impertinent.

A more serious thought came upon him. He returned to the cave.

CHAPTER 17

The News

HEROD WAS RESTLESS. His sleep was usually sporadic and unsatisfying, but this night he was literally without rest. No part of his body was free of pain. He had commissioned the bed himself, a stack of large thin mattresses filled with wool, with a cotton-stuffed mattress on top, a stack tall enough so that he could fall safely onto it at night and slide off in the morning.

This night he might as well have tried to sleep on a slab of marble. At least it would have been easier to roll and curl and stretch as he tried to quiet his joints and muscles, and, more and more these days, his insides.

This night he ended up on his side.

So it was that when he realized that sleep was not going to come, and he opened his eyes, the first thing he saw at the edge of his bed was the little Frog.

It was barely a silhouette in the room dimly lit by the moon filtering through the old shutters. Herod lay still, thinking the vision would resolve into some froggish shape of his bunched sheet or some unusual frolic of light and shadow at the hem of his blanket.

The Frog croaked.

Herod yelled and worked his arms free from his covers. He slapped at the Frog but she had disappeared into the dark. Herod flung off his covers and began to paw through them to find the invader. Nothing.

There she was, atop a post of the frame that held his bedding.

That devil frog mouth is still smiling!

Here to tell me something.

Herod lunged at her but his reflexes were no match for the Frog's, who was gone before the king had moved an inch.

The guard heard Herod holler and rushed into the bedchamber.

"What is it, my king?"

He was a good guard and did not wait for a response. He opened the shutter to let in the moonlight and stomped all around the room with sword drawn, but with no idea what threat he was supposed to be stalking.

Herod sat up. His pain had temporarily funneled into the concentration he had brought to bear on the little Frog, but it was returning.

"Nothing. Nothing . . . . "

The guard stopped his search and stood before Herod. He bowed.

"Bad dream," Herod said. "An undigested bit of

mutton." He tried to chuckle a little. The guard tried to chuckle a little.

The guard bade Herod good night. He told his king he would forego his rounds and would stand outside the door for the rest of the night.

"Your quick response is noted," Herod said. The guard bowed again. "Leave the shutter open." Perhaps the Frog would depart the way it must have arrived.

He rose from his bed and went to the window. He squinted at the full moon. *Is it throbbing?* He rubbed his forehead and wondered if he would ever feel good again.

And whether Ogen had completed his orders with those fancy foreign seers.

And where that wretched little Frog had gone.

And what news she brought.

CHAPTER 18

Mary's Song

THE CAVE WAS finally quiet. In the stable, Zac and Hannah lowered themselves to the ground and slept.

The moon was now high in the southern sky. Susannah tried to get Mary to sleep for a bit. Jesus required no such urging.

Joseph spoke to Sandar. "You're quiet."

"Being quiet seems like my best use right now."

"What is it?"

Sandar drew Joseph outside and away from the cave. "I must speak with you."

"You seem troubled even as our joy is finally upon us."

"Last night in Jericho I met three astrologers from foreign lands. They had told Herod that a sign that had come upon Jerusalem meant that there was a child somewhere who was destined to lead the Jews, perhaps all of Israel. They were to find this child and report back to Herod. They are traveling with Herod's armed guard. They said Herod had given them gold as a gift for the child. One of them mentioned prophecies."

Joseph said, "That they are looking at this time is another sign that Jesus is who we have dreamed he is."

Sandar realized he had not conveyed the concern – more than concern – he was feeling.

"Listen to me, Joseph. Armed men serving a jealous king of well-known ferocity would be a strange sign indeed, with or without magicians alongside. I didn't like the look of those soldiers, and I didn't like the insinuations I felt from the leader of the guard when I spoke to him. I can't say whether they would act contrary to the instructions of the magi, but I can tell you their first loyalty is to Herod."

"But you said Herod sent gold."

"That's what Herod told the magi, but I'm thinking the only thing that promise of gold bought him was their false belief in his good intentions. I'm telling you, Joseph – look at me – I'm telling you that Herod sees the king of the Jews every morning in his looking-glass!"

Joseph thought it over.

Sandar continued: "You should leave Bethlehem. Go south from here. I don't think Herod would reach into Egypt. If not in the morning, soon, as soon as Mary is able. Susannah and I can assist your journey, even accompany you south. We'll find donkeys for you."

Sandar waited for assent, but it was not forthcoming.

"The astrologers," Joseph said. "Do you believe they present a danger themselves? Are they conjurers?"

"The three men themselves seemed sincere in their search. And they were men who knew our God, although I can't be certain if He is the first god among others of their lands. But gold or no gold, no commission from Herod accompanied by armed soldiers is likely to have a good result for its target."

"It isn't our intention to stay long in Bethlehem," Joseph said. "Long enough for the *brit milah* –"

"Eight days!" Sandar said. "They were headed this way the same morning I left for Jerusalem."

Joseph said, "Mary has suggested to me – she's more than suggested, you know her – that we shouldn't return to Nazareth now. She couldn't say why, just one of her feelings that seem to be visited on her. But perhaps you're now suggesting the answer with your report of the encounter with Herod's guards."

"I no longer wonder at Mary's words," Sandar said.

"Perhaps they won't find us."

"The same thing that drew you to Bethlehem will call them here as well."

"They are of David?"

"No," Sandar said, "but if I know the Bethlehem prophecy, it's likely they know it as well. A babe in a cave out of a young girl in the city of David will excite them. They seek a sign, but here is the thing itself, or something that looks very much like it. Or at least something they can sell Herod. Or, God forbid it, something for the guard to – to act upon."

Joseph looked back past the stable into the cave in the hillside and Mary with the baby Jesus. Susannah was speaking to her. "I had not expected the world to know him so soon," Joseph said. "I'll tell Mary."

"She probably already knows."

"Nothing surprises me," Joseph said. "I'm only the father – but really not even . . . . "

"Susannah told me about – about Mary's –"

"You needn't say it," Joseph said. "It does me honor to be Mary's betrothed and the man who will teach Jesus the ways of men. When she told me, I was – I didn't know what to believe. At first, I confess to you before God, I thought her crazy, or fallen, even at her young age. But in dreams I learned the meaning of her words and I've trusted her and my dreams ever since. Then you appeared and saved us, and Susannah – what a treasure on earth your woman is! – joined us to ensure Mary's safety and guide her in these early days. And to bear witness to the prophecy as to Mary's . . . condition – as a woman. The Fox, the Lion! The sky and the land! I know now even more strongly that the prophecies are become real in this age through her."

He looked Sandar in the eye. "Builder," he said, "you must see – you *must* see – that the magi you met must find us. It's not the gold –"

"I didn't think –"

Joseph held up his hand. "I know. But we cannot hide the fulfilled prophecies from those who have been bold enough to believe in them."

"I understand your words," Sandar said, "and I admire your faith. I do. But I can't share your hope that Herod has issued the first benevolent orders of his life to this guard."

"I understand," Joseph said. "Neither you nor I expected such drama when we left Nazareth."

"Only two days ago," Sandar mused. "No matter. My

own journey, and Susannah's, remain yours until you're safe. Let's go tell Mary what may yet come to Bethlehem."

❧

They found Mary suckling Jesus. Susannah was speaking to her in low tones and occasionally reaching out to touch the baby's head under Mary's shawl.

"The menfolk have returned," Susannah said. "No doubt with some proposal on how to make themselves useful."

"On the contrary," Sandar said. "We await your own proposals on that subject."

Mary said, "Susannah, you chose your betrothed wisely. He'll be of value to your household, as he seems ready to do your bidding."

"And Joseph honors you in all things," Susannah said. "But I believe they've come to us with concerns other than who is to direct our households."

Sandar told Mary and Susannah about his encounter with the magi.

"Our dreams are proved with each passing hour," Joseph said.

"There is more," Mary said.

"There is," Sandar said. "Herod sponsors their search. His guard is with them. They claim to be protecting the magi, but Herod – he's murdered two of his *own* sons. I can't even speak what I'm fearing."

Mary turned to Joseph, who said, "I told him we would greet the magi should they visit."

"So we shall, my betrothed," Mary said.

"The guard," Sandar said, "they are hard men. They

are not sentimental about the prophecies and they worship kings and gold, not God. We do not know what orders they have."

"Will they not respect the magi?" Mary said.

"I don't know," Sandar said, "but I do know we're not talking about robbers who skulk in the forests and behind rocks. You can't risk the magi guessing that Jesus is the child they seek. They are desperate to find the special one they predicted. If they claim they have found him, sign or no sign, my blades and Joseph's tools, and even Susannah's animal cry to the pagan gods, will not protect Jesus from these soldiers if their orders are as I fear they may be. Even a lion would fall before their swords."

"We will abide the event," Joseph said. "You speak wisely as always, Builder. But the magi who read the skies must find us, and we must not run from them, no matter who is with them. And we must stay eight days for the *brit milah*."

Susannah said, "The *brit milah* may be held at any place, a place distant and hidden from here." She turned to Mary. "You have come so far, and endured so much, please . . . ."

Mary stood and placed Jesus in the manger. She straightened and faced Sandar and Susannah directly.

"God has not set His child before us, He has not brought us through our many hardships only to abandon him and us," Mary said. "Builder, I have come to understand that you spoke truly this morning when you referred to our journey as a story. A story that will outlive us all. Sometimes good things happen – you rescue us from the

robbers; sometimes bad – Jesus must be born among animals in a cold dark stinking cave. But the story cannot end
here. It cannot. Now that we know of the magi we know,
Joseph and I, that they are sent to be part of the drama of
these days and nights."

She looked down at Jesus.

"*Even the threat from Herod* – yes, Builder, we've heard
what you're saying – that's part of his story, too. We will
await their arrival."

"If they arrive at all," Sandar said. "Who knows where
they are, how long you will be required to live in this cave?"

"The story must happen before it may be told,"
Joseph said.

Susannah said, "Don't be beguiled by today's miracles
and the story in which you have found yourselves! Mary,
you have borne Jesus in Bethlehem as a maiden. The prophecy is fulfilled. Jesus lives; he is strong. Accompany us south
at sunrise."

"No," Mary said.

Susannah touched Sandar's arm, but the gesture was
unnecessary to quiet him. He saw that no amount of scolding or pleading was going to budge the family from the
cave.

"I haven't won an argument with you two yet," he
said. "If you won't get as far away from Jerusalem as possible, tomorrow Susannah and I can look for townspeople
of David's line who will be honored to take you in with a
newborn. And I'll insist that you allow me to make your
tenancy more attractive with an offer of some rent or a gift
to the syn–"

"No."

Susannah said, "Mary, don't be proud. Accept our help with the new day tomorrow."

"No," she said again, firmly but without emotion.

"We're all tired," Sandar said. "I suggest we sleep, perhaps in shifts, and consider these matters in the morning. I have a mat, Susannah brought one as well, Joseph had a couple in his pack, and we now have many blankets —"

"No!"

"Mary," Susannah said, "what are you telling us? It's time to rest, to sleep if we can. There is much to do tomorrow."

"This night's story is not over," she said. Her face was bright; her eyes gleaming with a new fire. "Hear the song of my heart!"

She said:

"Sandar and Susannah:

"You have seen what you have seen.

"You have heard what you have heard.

"You have felt what you have felt.

"You have known the truth of what your senses have told you about what has happened this day and night.

"You have come to know the satisfaction of the prophecies, and you have aided in their accomplishment in ways that not even Joseph and I had foreknown.

"You are now present as our destinies are fulfilled, and now it is the job of our lives – Joseph's and mine – to see that Jesus's destiny is realized.

"Your role in the story that has ended with the birth of Jesus has come to an end.

"Your own stories, which will be rich with love and satisfaction and glory, and which you will reach in the love of one another, begin now.

"But your stories cannot mingle with ours in this mean cave.

"You must leave us, and you must leave us tonight.

"You must leave now."

Sandar and Susannah were stunned at the bluntness of her refusals and demands. They did not require the couple's gratitude, but to be ordered to depart with the moon still bright felt very much like its opposite.

But Mary was not finished.

"Susannah, I see you're about to speak. Heed me, please.

"You and Sandar have provided miraculously and fully for us. Jesus is healthy. I'm strong, thanks to your care, and ready to care for Jesus thanks to your instruction. Our news will soon become known to others who will protect Jesus and Joseph and I until we can establish ourselves as a family again in Nazareth.

"Sandar, I told you today that your story is not finished. Although you gained betrothal to Susannah, it remains unfinished as your journey together continues. More chapters will be written this night, but not

here, where the glory of Jesus's birth is the sole blessing and drama of this cave.

"So tonight it must be, and now. The moon is high and the sky is clear and the road will be bright before you.

"Please do not think me high-handed in my manner. I have been merely a vessel, and, even delivered of Jesus, I am still. I know what I know and I cannot know less, and I cannot know otherwise. And I must speak it.

"The miracles of this this day and night are not over. I know this as surely as I know the son of man beloved joyfully of God sleeps in the manger Sandar and Joseph built from the trash of the inn."

Mary's voice rose.

"And I know that glory will be visited upon you! You will be risen up! You will be blessed with the love of this child, who will hear from us of your gifts of courage and kindness, and blessed as well with the love of many children, and their children, and the children of the ages.

"Go with our love and gratitude that is boundless and wordless. Go. Go now, with the blessings of all that you have seen and heard and felt this day and night."

Sandar was fearful that Susannah would speak sharply in rebuke. But she was quiet.

Mary said, "Go."

"Don't worry about us," Joseph said.

Mary took Susannah's face in her hands and looked deeply into her eyes.

Susannah said, "We will go."

Joseph said, "Sometimes I understand, sometimes I don't. She is a girl; but I've come to know that her words sound with the weight and wisdom of the centuries, and I say to you, Sandar the Builder and Susannah his betrothed, go. Go, and know with all the certainty that a simple carpenter of Nazareth can summon, that you will go in glory."

Susannah said again, "We will go."

Sandar had traveled with Joseph and Mary since the morning. He was not accustomed to being told what to do, but ever since he had routed the robbers earlier that day, he found himself hearing Mary's strangely confident pronouncements and requests – commands? — with confusion, then wonderment, then respect.

He smiled to himself at the absurdity of resistance.

"Two women have said it. One is the mother of God's son." He smiled and faced Susannah. She returned it.

"And the other – I fear. I'll prepare Zac and Hannah."

CHAPTER 19

Risen Up

"It's the middle of the night," Susannah said. "And here we are on the road out of Bethlehem as though we were going to market in the middle of the day."

Sandar had been quiet since they left Bethlehem. "I can't deny it, my betrothed. At least the moon is high and lends some guidance. And it gives the snow on the hills a lovely midday luster. Still, it's odd to be traveling this road at this time."

"So many shepherds," Susannah said.

"Birthing season," Sandar said. "The ewes are helpless when the lambs arrive."

"Birthing season indeed," Susannah said.

"Mary's lamb was some new thing, wasn't he?"

"I've helped dozens of little lambs into the world, but never one with his – I don't even know what to call it."

"When he touched me – he unlocked – he opened – I don't know, either. It was like the words were always here"

— Sandar thumped his chest — "something I knew, something I may even have been born with, but had forgotten."

Sandar stole a glance at the woman on the tall donkey next to him. So many gifts in a single day.

Susannah said, "You and I are both stubborn. But a girl weakened by childbirth ordered us away."

"And we complied without a word of objection."

"Yet I felt the rightness of it when she spoke."

Sandar chuckled. "I always try to be a good guest, which includes leaving."

"When I woke up this morning," Susannah said, "I didn't expect to be betrothed to a Gentile and yanking the son of God into the cold night air."

"I didn't expect to fight off robbers and restore a fox to life. Or be rescued by a lion."

"Or," he added, "be stunned in the heart by Nathan's touchy daughter."

"Many men have not expected that," she said, "and they have not been disappointed."

He said, "I suppose I should also mention attending the birth of the son of God among the things I was not expecting."

"You should."

"Just did." Sandar laughed. "I feel . . . I feel as though what has happened to me, to both of us, yesterday, tonight, has been entirely out of my hands. At least until you and I finally find our rest after all of this, my course is to do as the world suggests."

"As God suggests," she said.

"Mm. I never thought as God's word as a suggestion.

But yes." *This is what it means to be free. To be forced to believe honors nothing.* Sandar thought he might consider that further when he wasn't so chilly.

"For now, I give myself up to it with thanks for a strong donkey beneath me and a strong woman beside me."

"Not in that order, I hope."

"Never, Susannah."

They rode in silence for a little while.

Sandar said, "Why didn't I suggest to them that we would find them a room in the inn in the morning after the travelers had left? We could easily have done that, and left them money to pay for their needs. Why didn't I say or do that obvious and sensible thing?"

"I don't know," Susannah said. "I didn't think of it, either. And why would Mary resist finding a home friendly to David's descendant? It's like she and Joseph want to stay in that cave."

"I have wondered about that cave, the stable," Sandar said. "God, or something, stayed my mind and voice. It makes no sense, but little has proceeded according to nature and logic in my life – our lives – lately."

"Whatever the reason," Susannah said, "here we are, and there they are."

Sandar said, "I've trained myself to sleep while I ride when Zac needs no direction. Hannah seems content to go where Zac goes. Do you think you could at least rest your eyes without falling off?"

"Perhaps," she said. "Do you snore?"

"I don't know," Sandar said. "If I were less concerned about my personal well-being I would wonder why you thought to ask about the possibility of someone's snoring interrupting your sleep."

"Ha!" Susannah said. "It'll take more than a bawdy joke to provoke me. Father snores like thunder through stone walls, and, after a cup of wine, so does mother."

They both closed their eyes. In a few moments their bodies surrendered to the stresses of the day and night as they swayed gently atop Zac and Hannah.

They slept lightly but it was sleep.

❧

They woke at the same time. They did not know how long they had been asleep.

Zac and Hannah had halted.

Dim clouds, perhaps a dozen, appeared in the sky over the fields to the east. As they watched, the clouds grew larger and brighter as they descended to earth, and they gathered into a single crown of fog. Indistinct shapes moved through the cloud as it glittered and sparkled. The cloud settled over the scattered groups of shepherds, obscuring the men from the riders' view. They could hear faint shouts of alarm as the shepherds disappeared into the glow. Music flowed from the cloud, but its melodies and harmonies were unknown to them.

"What are we seeing?" Susannah said.

"What are we hearing?" Sandar said.

"It's like no song I've heard."

"It's like no song ever heard."

"It's strange but beautiful to the ear," Susannah said.

"The voices — are they women or men?"

"Neither, both. The words . . . seem to form out of the mist."

"Can you make them out?"

"So dim in the distance," Susannah said. "Yet clear enough, sometimes. The words tumble together, some are loud, some are soft, and I cannot discern phrases. It's hard to make out but so lovely and comforting to hear."

"Mary was right," Sandar said. "The wonders of the night follow us still."

They marveled to the music and strained after the words.

Bethlehem

Son

Tonight

Glory

Go

News

See

Praise

Eyes

Manger

God

Son

Hosannah

Stable

Inn

See

Eyes

Worship

Go

Baby
Hosannah
Messiah
Mankind
Cave
Tonight
Bethlehem
Swaddled
Messiah
Son
Joy
Glory
Peace
Goodwill
God
Son
Messiah
Go
Bethlehem
Go
Now

Zac and Hannah were unperturbed, waiting for whatever was next asked of them. Sandar and Susannah watched the shifting, glowing clouds in silence and listened to the song that rose from them.

The clouds began to dim and evanesce, eventually disappearing altogether as their song faded along with them. Sandar and Susannah could see the shepherds, huddled together in knots throughout the hillsides, many of them fallen to the ground or on their knees. Some cried out;

most were silent. They began to move uncertainly, the herding teams coming together in larger groups.

"They are gathering to talk about what they have seen and heard," Susannah said.

"What *have* they seen and heard?" Sandar said. "What have we? Perhaps they heard those voices as uncertainly as we did, unaccustomed as are our ears to words from the heavens."

Out of the corner of his eye Sandar caught Zac's ears prick skyward.

"Sandar!" Susannah cried. "The cloud has come for us!"

"There's no escape; let's be still and listen."

A cloud – they could not tell its size – descended over them. It was blinding bright and denser than fog. Sandar saw the donkeys' heads disappearing into the gathering light and in a moment he could not see his own hands or Susannah beside him.

"Don't be frightened," Sandar said. "Zac and Hannah are not sensing danger, and I feel a strange ease in its embrace."

"Yes," Susannah said. "I also feel a gracious, comforting presence. It's like light come alive. It's everywhere but I feel nothing against my skin, no smell, no sound as it moves. There are shapes within it but they're – they're loving, joyful."

"I wonder if they will have music for us," Sandar said.

Susannah said. "I can hear," but she stopped.

The harmonies were dense and startling and urgent, but words began to emerge from the music.

Star

Guide

Rise

Cloud

You

Fly

Cave

Light

Sign

The words arrived then faded, returned then retreated. Deprived of their senses save hearing in the swirling mist, Sandar and Susannah strained to hear.

Star

Stable

You

Guide

They struggled to put some grammar to the words, to learn what they were being told, but the shapes seemed all to speak at once.

Star

Sign

You

Cloud

Cave

Light

Go

And the cloud lifted vanished up into the dark sky.

Susannah gasped.

Sandar said, "Oh."

The donkeys still beneath them, and still calm, as the couple's eyes refocused from the soft infinity of the cloud, they found themselves high above the ground, floating without purchase to anything but the air, although strangely secure in the cold dark.

"Sandar!"

His mind raced, but he said, "Still, still, still."

Far below them the shepherds continued to mill about. They saw the men and boys gesturing dramatically to one another but could not make out the words of their excited exchanges. They could see Bethlehem and, Sandar thought, the faint glow of the stable and cave where the oil lamps still burned and Jesus was asleep.

Sandar laughed softly. "I say again, my betrothed, do not be frightened. Be steady on Hannah."

"Mary," Susannah said. "She said our destinies begin now, but not at the cave."

"Yes," Sandar said.

"I won't be fearful of what is to come," she said, but without much conviction.

"Nor will I," Sandar said, "but for now, I wouldn't think to dismount." He laughed softly again. "What happens next will become known to us, as it has all day and night. Let us be alive to our feelings on this night of nights."

Her common sense returned. "But Sandar! Donkeys cannot fl –"

"Sssh! Perhaps not, but I don't wish to suggest that to Zac. He's quite sensitive, and who knows whether his faith that all is normal is what's keeping us up here."

"This is hardly a laughing matter, my betrothed."

"Yes, yes, I know," Sandar said. "I don't mean to make light of our situation, but I do find it amusing that our path this day is out of our hands in what I'm coming more to think is a most delightful fashion. As intrigued and even perplexed as I am, I find myself quite inexplicably joyful. I'm almost giddy!" And he laughed.

"You won't be laughing if Zac starts to buck or Hannah trips over a meteor. Truly, Sandar, they cannot fly!"

Sandar continued to laugh as he spoke:

"And virgins cannot conceive!

"And foreign magicians cannot travel the whole of Israel in search of a child with a commission from Herod!

"And a dignified woman of Jerusalem cannot transform into a shrieking demon to threaten the cocks of lurking bandits, and the moon cannot disappear on a clear night!

"And the desert cannot explode into sparkling life before my eyes!

"And the same robbers robbing the same people twice can't be foiled twice in the same day!

"And a dying fox can't return to life and summon a lion who can tell the difference between robbers and innocent travelers!

"And a child cannot be born and laid in a manger made of wastewood created in a drunken riot the night before, hauled into the world by a midwife the mother had never laid eyes on and could not have expected to encounter, who meets the prophecies of the hundred years for Israel's savior! In a hole someone carved out of solid rock for no reason!

"And voices and songs never before heard by man cannot come from shining clouds from a cloudless sky!"

Sandar calmed down.

"And mark, Susannah: A man out of the stock of Greece and Rome and some stranger from the northlands could never expect to win the hand of the fairest maid of Jerusalem, eh? After my last day and night I'm not prepared to say that anything is impossible."

Susannah herself had to giggle. "Perhaps you're right to laugh. I thought we were normal people, yet here we are in the middle of this glorious day and night. You spoke truly this afternoon in my father's house," she said. "Our old ways seem useless now."

"The world itself has changed," Sandar said. "I've spent my life dreaming to be free of the earth, to be free of the works of men, to see it all! And today I've received the gift of the heavens and earth from a tiny baby."

They turned to face one another.

"Not to mention a most precious personal gift," he said, taking her hand. "My joys this day are all of a piece. Lean to me; carefully, now." Their kiss was short as the donkeys jostled beneath them.

They looked down at the shepherds, tiny but distinct below, and at the village not far off.

"We're turned around," Susannah said. "We face Bethlehem."

"Our first sign," Sandar said. "Zac!"

The donkey raised his head. Sandar gave his flanks a gentle nudge with his heels. "Go."

Zac and Hannah pawed at the air as naturally as if they were going to market on a hardpack road; they moved toward Bethlehem as the shepherds swarmed confusedly below.

Sandar noticed dim sparkles of reflected moonlight from something on the Jerusalem road, but they were too far distant to make out.

CHAPTER 20
Prophecy Denied

OGEN HAD FELT like a fool the entire time he was guarding the magi. They rode ahead on their gleaming Arabian stallions festooned with embroideries completely inappropriate for the dusty roads of Israel, and dressed in shining colorful robes and that ridiculous headwear. While he followed on a donkey that was only partly successful in dodging the horses' droppings, and sweated under armor that would never be tested by the pathetic roadway thieves who only attacked pathetic travelers. And his mood curdled further when he finally realized where this unexpected left turn was taking them. He kicked his donkey to draw even with Melchior.

"The men were expecting to be in Jerusalem tonight, but there's nothing on the end of this road but Bethlehem, and Hebron after that!"

"It's not far and we won't be there long," Melchior said.

"Too long not to have to stay there the night, unless you plan to search in the dark."

"Our inquiries tomorrow will go swiftly," Melchior said. "Then your men can return to Jerusalem and its debaucheries."

"You secretly plot to bypass Jerusalem," Ogen said, "and now you insult the honor of Herod's guard!"

"You think we don't know what you say to your men? You think we don't know how you mock us and plot to haul us back before Herod? Is that your idea of honor? You want honor, honor the orders Herod gave you."

Ogen snorted. "There will be no room for our party there and we'll have to set the tents in this dark. Then a day of searching in Bethlehem, and for what? I don't think you know."

Old Caspar rode over. "If we knew what we were looking for, and where it was, we would have told Herod and saved ourselves and you a lot of trouble, taken our commission and gone home. We're not any more comfortable on this journey than you are. Herod was satisfied that our reading of the sky frogs was strong. Would you interrupt the quest he set for us?"

"You set this quest for yourselves and sold it to Herod like a toothless mule! Here we are, Herod's elite guard, protecting overdressed wizards from Arabia or India and" – he jerked his head toward Balthazar – "wherever this one is from, on a search for a dead myth! The priests you visit laugh at you when you leave. The people you question have no use for star men in hats worth more than their homes!"

Balthazar said, "The prophets suggest Bethlehem. Our visit there is worthwhile."

"Beh," Ogen spat. "A fine place for a king to emerge.

The place is scarcely more than a collection of huts and stables, some taverns where the shepherds go to drink when they start talking to the sheep."

"King David was born there," Balthazar said.

"Everyone has to be born somewhere. He left it and when he did the place went to sleep and never woke up."

"Herod believes in the prophets," Melchior said.

"Herod believes in Herod," Ogen said, "and so do I. "The prophets spoke centuries ago. Their heads were full of kings and vengeance and predictions that the priests make their livings repeating. Fantasies! Tell me, did the Hebrew prophets, or the stars, or perhaps an infestation of salamanders, predict Alexander, or the Caesars, or *anything, ever*? Did they prophesy Herod the Half-Jew would rule the Jews?"

"Herod was raised a Jew," Old Caspar said. "I'll tell him you called him that."

"You won't get that opportunity, if it comes to that," Ogen said. "Perhaps Herod is the king of the Jews, but to me he is the king of all the lands of Israel. And he is a king I fear. And one with Rome's support."

"If you fear him," Melchior said, "let us finish –"

"There is nothing to finish!" Ogen said. "And each of you knows it! You look for a ghost, a spirit, some vision in the heads of old men of the hundredyears. You'll have nothing for Herod but a story, something you dreamed up that my men won't support. It will be your heads."

Some of the other guards and hands heard this conversation. Several of them called out "Jerusalem!" and "Ogen speaks for us."

Ogen heard a sound. He looked up and saw – was it? It had to be the Heron silhouetted for the briefest moment against the moon.

Ogen raised his hand and the camels and donkeys stopped. The astrologers on their horses continued for a few tentative steps, but they stopped, too.

"We're turning around," Ogen said. "We're going to Jerusalem and you're coming with us. You may pretend to search *there* for all the good it will do you! I'll sleep well there tonight! And tomorrow night, and the night after!"

The guard and attendants cheered and began to turn the donkeys and camels around.

Balthazar dismounted and ran back after Ogen on his donkey.

"Truly, Ogen, one morning is all we need in Bethlehem and we can be in Jerusalem before sundown tomorrow. The prophecies –"

Ogen whirled to face him. "If you believed in the prophecies, you would have *started* in Bethlehem!"

Melchior and Old Caspar watched the donkeys and camels turning and walking back towards Jerusalem. Balthazar, greatly saddened, looked down at his moon-shadow on the road.

As he looked at the cold grey image on the ground before him, his mouth fell slowly open and his eyes grew wide at something he was not expecting to see.

A second shadow.

CHAPTER 21

The Sign

"Why are we here?" Sandar said.

"Ask Aristotle," Susannah snorted.

"You know what I mean. I mean why are we high above the road from Bethlehem, halfway to the firmament, practically spying on the shepherds, who can't see us in the dark at this height?"

"You're asking me?" Susannah said. "This was your journey today! I joined you as your betrothed and I must say it's been as interesting as you promised. But I'm also mystified as to why we're floating around up here, and now that I've gotten used to it, I'm equally mystified as to why it doesn't seem any more frightening than it does."

Sandar said, "I feel the same same. No fear has followed me up into the heavens. It seems as if we belong up here." He looked at the moonwashed earth. "It's as beautiful as I imagined."

"Surely we'll have to come down sometime," Susannah said. "We have to eat, sleep, live our lives."

Sandar was quiet for a moment, thinking. "Could it be that we're only characters in someone's dream? In my own dreams I've soared into the air and moved across the face of the world. Do you think that perhaps we're . . . not real?"

Susannah punched him hard in the arm.

"Ow, hey!" he said.

"Not real, you say. How would you judge that blow?"

"I judge it real enough," Sandar said.

"If we're in someone's dream I intend to scream and wake them."

"For the sake of our current elevation," Sandar said, "I urge you not to upset whatever host has suspended us up here, because, whether real or not, surely something has embraced us in its goodwill which we would not want to disturb with a shriek that might be interpreted as, shall we say, criticism."

"God?"

"Who else did you have in mind?"

"Best to keep my peace, then."

"Mm."

They floated toward the sky above Bethlehem, only a slight chill breeze disturbing the peace of their path.

The sparkle he had seen earlier on the highway had grown sharper as they moved north. "What's that party on the Jerusalem road?" Sandar said. "Can you make it out?"

"It looks like a group of military men," Susannah said. "It's difficult to identify it in the moonlight, but there also appear to be a few men on – are those horses? Yes, horses. And there are camels and donkeys. The men on the horses

— there are three. Their garments must be ornate, perhaps jeweled, they catch the moonlight."

"Yes!" Sandar said, "It must be the magi I met last night in Jericho with Herod's guard, the party I warned Joseph and Mary about. Their quest is almost at an end."

Susannah said, "Their quest may be ending sooner than you think. It looks like the entire party is turning back toward Jerusalem."

"No!" Sandar said. "Surely . . . ."

"What?"

What indeed? We're floating high off the earth. Is this the destiny Mary believed was ours?

He reached out for meaning, tried to imagine what possible destiny awaited them in the cold night air above the earth below and the firmament above, tried to look ahead to how the night must end, a story that was threatening to end before its final scenes had played.

Sandar said, "The shepherds are confused. They start to Bethlehem and then stop to argue. Some turn back. The magi and their party are now heading the wrong way."

"Sandar . . . ."

"*These things cannot be!*"

Zac and Hannah were slowing.

"Susannah!" Sandar said. "The story! There must be a story! I grasped it — so dimly! — this morning when I spoke to them on the road. It's as Mary said! When he comes into his destiny there must be tales to tell of this glorious night! An extraordinary story of the moment he joined us in the world! A story to remember! To celebrate! People must be there, must see it, must tell it! Look below!"

They saw a soft glow from the cave where they had left the family. They were directly above it, still too high to be seen against the dark sky. Zac and Hannah obeyed Sandar's order to halt.

"The shepherds must go as the music of the clouds commanded them. The magi must find the child they each predicted. We, alone of all the world, see that those stories are failing. We must save them. We're the only ones who can."

"The words I'm about to say are going to sound strange, even to me," Susannah said, "but there is logic in what you say, if anything at all may be said to be logical about flying donkeys floating over the birthplace of the newborn son of God. But what can we do? They can't see us in the dark or hear us clearly from this distance. If we screamed it would only frighten them, even if they could hear us, and it might spook our animals."

"You're right," Sandar said. "I've heard your scream."

Susannah said, "The moon is high but is in the southern sky, and its light is dim and mute and spread over the countryside."

"That's it," Sandar said.

"What's what?"

"The cave. It had to be the cave. They can't be in a closed room hidden away somewhere, an inn, or even a friendly home! Jesus must be found! He had to be born outdoors! The shepherds and magi cannot be puzzling over what is within buildings and walls and doorways. They must come freely to him! Joseph – and you, and Mary – were right. It was the perfect place for him to be born, and for us to –"

They saw it at the same time. A small cloud had appeared nearby and floated their way. It glowed faintly in the moonlight as nightclouds will.

Sandar began to laugh as the understanding struck him like a thunderclap:

"And he had to be born at night!"

He swung his legs around and faced backwards on Zac.

"What are you doing?" Susannah said. "This is no time for trick donkey riding. I didn't think you would lose your mind so soon after our betrothal."

Still laughing, louder now, he opened the bags that had been draped over Zac's rump and reached into them. "Your old friend the moon needs some help," he said. "Her beams need to be collected, connected, and redirected."

Sandar laughed again at his silliness; Susannah snorted and shook her head at this new madness of her betrothed. When he straightened, one hand was full of gold and silver pieces; the other, rubies and emeralds and diamonds and glass jewelry of every color.

The little cloud drew closer.

"Zac told me not to give these back to the bandits!" he said, and laughed again as he tossed them into the cloud. "Donkey bellies may not be visible from below, but look!"

The coins and jewels disappeared into the little cloud where they caught and reflected the moonlight, brightening it to its borders.

Sandar urged Zac slightly ahead so the bags of coins and jewels drew even with Susannah.

"Grab as much as you can and throw it in," Sandar said. "Quick, now! As much as you can, as fast as you can.

Rid us of this useless wealth – old wealth! – and let this heavenly cloud guide our friends below in the dark!"

Susannah paused to admire the beauty of the glittering cloud before she grabbed her own handfuls and tossed them cloudward.

Sandar howled and whooped. "Look at it!" he said. "Have you ever seen anything so beautiful?" Even the lowly brass coins seemed to shine with pride as they snagged the moonbeams and fed the little cloud's glow.

The cloud stretched to hold the moonlight captured by the spinning, flipping coins and jewels. It began to grow to something that no longer seemed quite a cloud, but a thing new in itself, a light that shone ever brighter and larger as they continued to feed it the shiny adornments of man the robbers had stolen. A Star it was become, but a new kind of star, a star come to earth with a true message.

As if it could hold no more light, the Star began to erupt in fizzing, sizzling streams and trails of green and red and gold shooting from it in all directions and falling earthward, the colors threaded throughout a cone of light that reached down to the stable and cave.

"Do you hear that?" Susannah said.

"Voices, but no words."

"With the same beauty we heard in the pastures."

Their four hands worked in harmony. They could not take their eyes off the vision of dancing colors combining in a blinding whiteness. Sandar's laughter mixed with the heavenly song.

The spectacle inspired them to even greater haste, great handfuls of coins and gems and jewelry, one after another.

There seemed no bottom to the bags-full of bandits' booty fueling the beacon, and when it seemed the Star could grow no brighter it shook and shed its borders, pouring brightness into the sky and challenging heaven itself. The rubies and emeralds and coins and all the rest gave up the beams they had seized from the moon, pouring them into a towering fall of light toward the nursery far below, bathing it in a warm and welcoming glow.

The Star, still glowing, still rumbling and popping, hung in the sky next to Sandar and Susannah like a benign and comforting storm.

Sandar laughed loud and long, breathless with joy.

CHAPTER 22

A New World

JOSEPH SAT WITH Mary at the back of the shallow cave. They looked down into Jesus's face as she held him while he slept.

The stable and cave-mouth were suddenly awash with a bright but soft glow from above. Joseph stepped outside the cave to see the enormous sun-bright Star directly above, blinding at its core but shooting colorful light in all directions.

"Mary, come see," he said.

She smiled but stayed seated with Jesus. "It's the Star," she said.

"Can you hear?" Joseph said.

"I hear."

"That's – is that –? It can't be."

"Why not, my betrothed? You've come to know many miracles."

"Sandar," Joseph said. "Our great friend, laughing with the angels."

"Our great friend," Mary said. "But, I think, perhaps no longer Sandar."

"And Susannah?"

"Changed also."

Joseph's heart was full. "And we are no longer the same, are we?"

Mary smiled her Mary-smile.

"None of us," Joseph said.

Smiling, both, at one another.

"The world," he said. "And all above and below it."

She came to the cave-mouth, covering Jesus's head with his blanket. She let the celebrating light wash her face in its glow, breathing in the song and laughter from on high.

"What is Sandar to become?" Joseph asked.

"There are many ways to bring joy to the world," she said.

She looked from Jesus to the Star.

"The children will believe," she said. "The children will come to him."

Jesus began to wake with gentle baby sounds, as if the next act were about to begin.

CHAPTER 23

A Star for the Magi

THE SECOND SHADOW.

Balthazar felt a thrill rising from his belly.

This was not a shadow of the moon, which had risen bright and full in the east and was now halfway across the sky. This shadow was shorter, from some light nearer-above and behind him. It flickered but was sharp against the sand-pack of the road.

Balthazar spun and looked into the sky. "It's the sign!" he said. "It's – is it a star?"

Old Caspar and Melchior had already turned. They had seen the departing backs of Ogen's men and animals suddenly light up.

The Star shone and flashed brilliantly high before them. There were colors, red and green, coming off the blinding core of pure whiteness and laced among the silver and gold flashes that were dancing in the sky and leaving trails in the astrologers' eyes.

"It's immense," Old Caspar said. "Like a cloud become sunlight. It's like no star I've ever seen."

"This is no storm, no lightning," Melchior said. "No thunder. No rain."

The cone of light from the Star to somewhere in Bethlehem grew brighter.

"It's like a star atop a tree of lights," Old Caspar said.

The three men watched in silence.

Ogen and his men had seen the road before them light up and had turned to look at the light. They were frozen with fear. Two of the men had begun to weep, and a couple of the young men had started to run away.

But to the magi the light was beautiful, and it delighted and comforted them as they understood instantly why this gigantic rainbow star had appeared. But there was also about the light a kind of violence, a heavenly lantern that flashed a message that the old ways would be wrenched aside, crowded out by whatever was inspiring this stunning vision in the sky. Melchior noticed that the animals seemed unafraid, even though the suddenly illuminated road and landscape exploding out of the dark must have been strange to them.

"The sign!" Balthazar said. "It has come to Bethlehem!"

"As will we," Old Caspar said. "Ogen! Tell your men not to be afraid. Be like your donkeys and camels."

He need hardly have spoken. The astrologers' horses willingly turned around and continued south down the road, as the fierce light was beckoning. Even without a command the guard's camels and donkeys did the same and walked unafraid toward Bethlehem, even as their masters remained shocked with the sky aflame ahead of them.

The giant erupting Star rose ahead of them as they put their heels to their Arabians and raced to Bethlehem. Melchior was fearful that it might disappear as quickly as it had appeared. The magi were watchers of the skies, but none of their experience was with this – what? A hole in the firmament? It was as if heaven itself was shining through.

The Star was too bright to stare at directly for very long. With each new glance it seemed to take on a different shape and feature a different hue at its core. Was it alive? Was it natural? Was it of this world?

Melchior shook his head to clear it. He had been weary; they had not rested since Jericho that morning. The appearance of the Star had shocked all three of them back to full waking. *No* to all that. This was the sign they had begun to despair of finding. It was of the God of the Jews.

"It's stopped over the town," Balthazar said. "The prophet is justified!"

They had reached the first small huts of Bethlehem.

Old Caspar said, "Balthazar, run with your young legs to find where it's at zenith."

"Hold up!" Melchior ordered. "Be still! Listen!"

"I hear it," Balthazar said. "So faint, but it's of the Star."

"Is it speaking?" Old Caspar asked.

"It's – is it? – it's laughing!" Balthazar said. And he laughed himself.

They all heard the faint yet deep and rich explosion of joy that went on and on.

"The laughing," Balthazar said, "it's embedded in a swirl of other voices. It's a song like none heard in Aegyptus."

"Or Arabia or any land I've visited," Melchior said

"A double sign, of sight and of sound," Old Caspar said.

Melchior said, "I've heard that laugh before."

CHAPTER 24

The Town

EZRA'S THOUGHTS JUMPED from one to the next without reason as he was drifting off to sleep, but the one thought that kept looping through his doze was: *I need to refit that shutter.*

Until he thought: *Why am I thinking about refitting that shutter?*

He opened his eyes. Light was flickering around the edges of the shutter and through some cracks in the wood.

He hoisted himself up on an elbow and tried to wake up.

His wife Naomi was sensitive to Ezra's comfort, and when he rose she paused her slide into sleep as well.

"What is that?" she said.

"Do I want to know?" he said. "There's never been such a light here."

Ezra went to the door of their home and looked out. Men from the village had gathered in the broad street and were looking up in the sky. A few women stood in door-ways. There was something odd about the illumination of the street. The moon was never so bright, and it didn't flicker. And the men were facing away from it.

"I'll be back," Ezra said. That seemed obvious, but he thought he needed to say something to Naomi, who would worry.

Ezra joined the group of men who were looking up at the Star and the cascading light appearing to come to ground some blocks away.

No sounds of destruction could be heard. The light stayed where it was. There was sound, too, but the men could not make it out. The cone of light hosted rivers of other colors, green, red, gold. Several of the men, among the more devout of the community, had gone to their knees.

An old priest from the synagogue joined the men.

One of the townsmen said, "What is it, teacher?"

The old priest had been nodding quietly. He seemed pleased to see the light.

"The God who spoke to our people and slaughtered the unlawful has been silent for four hundred years," he said. "Perhaps he is clearing his throat."

∽

Ezra walked into their house past Naomi, who had stopped short of the open doorway to peek fearfully out at the gathering.

He sat at the table. He looked straight ahead.

"Is there wine?"

Naomi poured some wine into a cup and set it before him.

"Thank you, my wife."

He took a long swallow.

He said, "Please tell your mother she may stay with us as long as she wants."

CHAPTER 25

The Visitors

THE FIVE APPROACHED the stable from the street with small steps. Joseph saw two men, two older boys, and a young boy. They stopped at the mouth of the alley between the stable and the inn that led to the cave. They were dressed warmly and smelled of woodsmoke and raw wool. Each held a shepherd's crook about a man's height or a little more. Even under their garments they looked muscled and rough, but they approached quietly and with caution. And, Joseph perceived, a little fear, as they glanced up at the spitting, singing, laughing light.

"Welcome," Joseph said.

"We heard a song in a cloud of light that fell on us," the larger of the two men said. "We didn't understand all of it. And we were afraid. But the words were of a special child born in the town this night and bade us visit."

The second man said, "When we didn't know where to go, we saw the light in the sky, brighter than the moon."

The five visitors and Joseph all looked up to see the exploding light.

The young boy said, "Hear! The light itself expresses joy."

Joseph nodded. "Yes," he said, "we have heard it."

"I'm Eli," the first man said. I'm with Caleb and his sons Asher and Aaron. The boy Tobias is mine."

"I am honored," Joseph said.

Eli said, "Is there a child within?"

"Yes," Joseph said. "Please follow me back to the cave and join us. We'll be pleased to share our own joy with you."

Joseph started back to the cave but saw that only the boy was with him. "Please come," he said. "It's just a baby and his mother, and he's sleeping. There's nothing within to fear. As you can hear, the Star is happy with what has taken place here."

The men shuffled behind Joseph, still confused from what they saw and heard in their fields and unsure of what they were to encounter.

"Welcome, men of the fields," Mary said to them. "This is Jesus."

"It's a baby, Caleb," Eli said, addressing the second man.

"So we were told by the light on the hills," Caleb said.

"Is he special?" Eli asked. "Do not misunderstand me. I'm joyful for your good fortune in the birth of this healthy boy."

"There was a song and a laughing Star," the young boy said. "That's special enough for me." He dropped to his knees and looked at Jesus more closely. He found his hands clasped naturally before him.

"I heard the word *messiah* in the cloud's song," Asher

said. "Is this the Messiah? Will he be our king? Is he now the king?"

Mary said. "It is beyond my power to declare. Men will either believe, or they will not."

"I heard it, too," Aaron said. "The words flew around us but the birth of the Messiah is what they were sending us to find, that's what I felt in the words." He fell to his knees.

"And so we have found it," Eli said, "if we believe." He and the other two went to their knees.

Jesus woke up. His eyes were clear and seeing.

"Hey," the boy said. "I'm Tobias."

Jesus looked up at him.

"He smiled at me!" Tobias said.

Joseph said, "He's pleased to see you."

Eli said, "We're men and boys of no great learning. We see many unusual things in the fields at night, many things that can trick the eye and lead the mind astray. But we five, and certainly many others on nearby hills, all saw the light and felt the warmth and the song, a song like none other we had heard. The words told us of the birth of a boychild, a boychild who was a savior, and we saw the Star and came to it, and here is a boychild."

"But you're wondering," said Joseph, "that the glory you have seen and heard has led you to a cold cave and this rough bed and nothing at all royal or powerful about any of it, or about his mother and me."

"Forgive me," Eli said. "Yes. I'm wondering at that."

There was a sound of running feet outside the stable. Suddenly a young man appeared at the cave, out of breath, his eyes large. His skin was darker than any Judean any of them had seen, near black in the light from the oil lamps. He was richly dressed, with a fine jeweled turban he was holding on his head. He spotted Jesus in the manger and, without a word, turned and ran back the way he had come.

Caleb said, "Well, Eli, that's not someone likely to visit a cold nursery in the middle of the night. Maybe we'll encounter royalty after all."

Soon Joseph heard a shuffling of feet and hooves and voices outside the stable and left to investigate. He returned with three men dressed in fine coats that parted to reveal rich tunics beneath – one old and fat, one young and lithe – the one who had appeared a few moments earlier – and a man of middle years whose stride and look bespoke authority.

"I am Melchior," the last of the three said. "Accompanying me this night are Caspar, the wisest man of my acquaintance, and Balthazar, a young scholar whose guidance has been invaluable on our journey through these lands. He visited you briefly a short time ago."

Joseph said, "You're the scholars of the stars whose arrival we were expecting. Sent by Herod, we heard."

Melchior was startled. "Where did you hear such a thing?"

"We were blessed to encounter Sandar the Builder of Nazareth," Mary said. "He said he had met three noble and learned men who were seeking a special child and were hoping for a sign."

"Sandar!" Balthazar said.

"Signs upon signs," Old Caspar observed. "Is he here?"

"No," Mary said. "He was with us today and tonight but he has departed."

"With the moon his only guide?" Old Caspar said.

Mary said, "Sandar is a man called to ride the night with many tasks to perform."

Melchior whispered: "Here he is." He moved carefully toward the tiny manger. "May I approach? I do not wish to presume too much," he said. "Is the child a boy?"

Joseph said, "His name is Jesus. Please join us, all of you."

"'He who will deliver us,'" Balthazar said, "'he who shall rescue.'"

The three men stood astonished at the sight of Jesus.

The magi had traveled the length and breadth of Israel meeting scorn and puzzlement from the people of whom they inquired. But they had come to understand that their greatest obstacle was the fear that Herod's name summoned. Three wizards on big horses with their rainbow garments, armed and armored men, a bizarre inquiry about some kind of magic boy, backed by a king who killed some of his own sons and was never, it seemed, going to die – best to smile, offer the men and their guard wine and bread, and shake their heads *we know of no such child.*

Despite their assurances to one another that they would find the child, in their private moments each regretted their reading of the frogs from the heavens as a metaphor for a prophecy realized, and regretted more deeply their response to Herod's summons in the hopes of a commission. They prayed for signs, but they knew the truth: the stars didn't move, the planets were predictable, and true heavenly signs were rare to the point of myth – Balthazar had never seen one, Melchior had misread one, and Old

Caspar couldn't remember one. Their journey, begun with optimism, threatened to end before an erratic and vengeful king, and no special child.

They each expected to die.

But here he was. Jesus. The messiah of the hundred-years foretelling. The metaphor become manifest. Under their eyes at arm's-length in a room entirely open to them. Under a Star that could not have been more of a sign. A shopkeeper could have read it.

Balthazar said, "I – I –" He could say no more. He fell to his knees next to Tobias. Melchior took Eli's place on his knees at the manger.

"I fear that if I should kneel I might never rise," Old Caspar said. "But I assure you that my honor to the child is no less than that of my fellows who are more limber than I."

Some of the stabled animals, donkeys and oxen, had awakened at the commotion of the visitors and were moving about at their tethers, confused at the noises in the dark hours. An unstabled goat and a large dog had wandered into the cave and, finding nothing to eat in the long stone manger, settled onto the ground. The visitors could not take their eyes from Jesus, who was now fully awake but also quiet, looking around his small bed at the faces who had gathered around him.

Melchior said, "You are shepherds."

"We are," Eli said. "Eli and Caleb and sons."

"You saw the Star."

"We did, but also a choir as if from heaven, telling us of this event."

"The Star has begun to fade," Balthazar observed. "It brought us all here; its purpose is now done."

Old Caspar had been thinking. He began to chuckle. He shook his head and laughed down into his beard, coughed twice, and laughed a little louder.

"My friends," he said.

Melchior and Balthazar looked up at him.

"We are said to be learned," Old Caspar said. "But we have been fools."

Melchior nodded. "I've felt it this night."

"As have I," Balthazar said.

"We were never to find this child inquiring among the learned and wealthy of Judea and Galilee and even Samaria," Old Caspar said. "At the synagogues we might as well have interviewed the floor."

"Yes," Melchior said. "Yes, it's so." Almost under his breath, as though finally believing some obvious thing for the first time, he said: "He was never to be of the cities, of the fine families, of any place believing itself fit to welcome the likes of us and pretending to hear our inquiries."

"Mark me," Old Caspar said. "Mark me as I say to you that we men of the stars wasted our time inquiring of the old stars that rise every night where we might find the savior of the prophecies," he said. "They held no answer for us, ever."

"Only the new Star spoke to us," Balthazar said.

Old Caspar rubbed the rich embroidered fabric of his robe between his fingers. "These raiments," he said. "They embarrass me as I sit here among the honest finery of Joseph and Mary and the shepherds." He craned his neck to look into the manger. "And the glorious swaddling of this beautiful child. I am naked, I tell you, naked beside him."

Melchior said, "This hole in a rock is greater than any throne room."

"Our hillsides by moonlight shame any palace," Caleb said.

"It had to be as this," Melchior said.

Old Caspar said, "Something new, not beholden to what he finds here, or even to the old – the old wisdom. Wisdom, heh. Not even beholden to old men like me."

He smoothed his rumpled robe. "A savior must be free of what he's saving us from."

Melchior looked around the cave, gesturing to the walls of stone. "He comes from the earth, as he does from Mary."

"And from the heavens, too," Balthazar said. "The laughing Star."

"Ha!" Old Caspar said. "Perhaps it was mocking us. And right to do so."

"Or happy to guide us to the good news," Melchior said. "It brought worthy Eli and Caleb and their fellows, too."

Old Caspar nodded into his beard and said, "Others may not think the news is good."

"Herod," Balthazar said.

"Herod, indeed," Melchior said. He rose; his eyes were hard. "We need to tend to the men who accompanied us," he said.

"Did they even follow us?" Balthazar said.

Old Caspar said, "They had to. Their animals turned around to follow the Star like it was speaking to them. Like our horses shed their fatigue when they saw it. I'm sure they're near."

Melchior said, "My defense of Herod was ill-considered," and he left the cave.

"What has Herod to do with this?" Caleb said. He rose and stood with Eli and the two older boys. "I don't like the sound of that."

Balthazar said, "We travel with a guard of Herod's. Don't be alarmed. I sense my friend Melchior has a plan. Let us handle Herod's men."

Melchior returned with Ogen, who was not pleased to be pulled into the cave. He had been watching the Star and even as it faded the fear grew within him that the star men had found a king to challenge the Herods.

"Come in here, Ogen, don't be afraid," Melchior said. "These men are shepherds. Joseph and Mary there are the parents of this baby here in this bed that looks like it might fall apart at any moment. The baby was born this night."

Ogen stared down at Jesus and looked around at the group in the stable. The mean setting and the shabby onlookers revived his bravado. "A baby," he said. "A baby in a cave. On a frozen night in a town that went to bed at sundown and would blow away in a spring *khamsin*. Attended by men with the stink of sheep on them." The shepherds started but Balthazar raised his hand and gave them a look asking them to calm.

"As you see," Old Caspar said.

"This is what you sought?"

"Look at him," Old Caspar said. "Look at them."

"You've found nothing," Ogen said. "As I predicted. A

king. A king! A king who fouls his blanket and wallows in it! Worshipped by oxen good only for the yoke." He spat.

"I regret that our journey with you has come to this," Melchior said. "I've consulted with Old Caspar and Balthazar and we have determined to bring our search to an end. We'll be leaving here tonight with sufficient provisions and animals for a journey, and we'll return to our homelands by a southern route. You may return to Jerusalem and Herod."

"What am I to tell Herod?"

"Tell him that sometimes a bunch of frogs is only a bunch of frogs," Old Caspar said.

"I don't care what you tell him," Melchior said. "Tell him the stars failed us. Tell him Judean frogs are less reliable than Arabian frogs. Tell him we misunderstood the prophecies. We would not be the first, and, I daresay, we will not be the last in these difficult times where men cling to vague promises from the ages when God spoke to men."

Old Caspar said, "The gold Herod sent with you, return it to him. Whether all of it reaches him – well, that's up to you. Myself, I don't know how careful the palace bursars are about disbursements from his treasury, but with the turmoil in Jerusalem . . . ."

"Herod will be furious at your failure," Ogen said.

"That's our problem," Melchior said. "You've served, and served faithfully, and we're grateful for your patience in what must have seemed a –"

"A fraud and a cheat on Herod!" Ogen said. "And now you seek to flee! I believe I'll take you back to Jerusalem."

"As you wish," Melchior said. "We'll tell him ourselves. He's probably forgotten all about us."

The Heron. "He has not."

"He won't be furious. He'll be happy when you report we found no new king. And we're returning the gold you're holding."

"You don't offer Herod back our wages," Ogen said.

"He would have had to pay those wages if you had been sitting on your asses in the palace," Old Caspar said. "Which, I might add, is not such a safe place to be sitting on your ass in these ass-threatening times. Are you on good terms with the sons Herod has allowed to live? And with his other guards, the ones he kept close to him while he sent you away with strangers, how do you get on with them?"

"Wait," Ogen said. "Wait." He looked fiercely around the cave. "I'm not stupid. You haven't said this is *not* the child you sought. The Star!"

"What star?" Old Caspar said, his face clean of guile.

Ogen stepped outside the cave and looked up into the empty sky. "It was just there. The Star that brought us here! You thought it was a sign! You're readers of the stars! It *was* a sign! This is the king you sought, in this stinking cave! This is the foretold savior of the Jews, wretched though he may be!"

"And if he is?" Melchior said. "You're prepared to return to Herod to tell him that our search was successful?"

"I have my own orders from Herod," Ogen said. "Finally, the star men I've been following all over Israel have found the child claimed to rule the Jews, even Herod and the sons of Herod!"

"We've made no such claim," Balthazar said. "And what do you know of the prophecies you mock?" he said.

"I know what Herod knows," Ogen said, "and he knows what you know because you filled his head with the prophecies when you sought your commission."

"This is a poor baby of poor parents," Melchior said. "You tell Herod a beggarly newborn will displace him and his brood and he'll laugh you out of the palace as he summons his executioners. Go home to Jerusalem. There's no threat to Herod here." *Oh, but there is, to all Herods and Caesars and those who would make them gods and seek the world's thrones.*

"Liar," Ogen said, menacingly. "You're all liars."

Balthazar stood. "Ogen," he said, "what is your commission from Herod?"

"That is no business of yours," Ogen said. "But it's discharged as surely on this child as on a king, whoever he may be."

"A moment ago you were terrified of the light that brought us to this child," Old Caspar said. "You would now seek to challenge the power of the God that sent that Star and set it here above this cave and stable? You would raise your sword against a helpless infant? No wonder Herod fears for his throne, with the likes of you standing guard!"

"Did you ever think that perhaps that Star wanted *me* to find the child?" Ogen said.

"No," Old Caspar said, "and neither did you when you were struck dumb by its appearance and could not wait to scurry back to Jerusalem with the rest of the rats that fear the light! People say they cannot see God, but I tell you, you see Him in this manger and in the sky above us this very night! You're right to fear Him and His wrath if you murder this child!"

"Herod is my god and star enough for me, old man! And I fear him above some fleeting, giggling light in the sky that has already vanished and this pup still wet from the womb!"

Ogen drew his sword and took a step toward the manger.

In the next instant, the crook end of a shepherd's staff appeared around his neck, and then another; and another around his ankles. And the stick end of a fourth at his groin.

"Put him down," Eli said.

Caleb yanked on the crook around Ogen's ankles. His feet left the cave floor and he fell flat on his back, the crooks held by the two older boys intact around his neck.

Eli pushed his staff into Ogen's crotch.

"Drop your sword," Eli said. "You and your men will not harm this baby or anyone else tonight."

Joseph said, "Are you the shepherds who destroyed the tavern at the inn last night?"

Caleb and Eli shared a look.

"Some of our friends may have been present," Caleb said.

"You're fools!" Ogen said. "Idiots! I have a dozen men out there all with swords and they will deal with five, five – herdsmen, and with bloody dispatch! Two men and three boys with . . . branches!"

"You have great confidence in that sword," Eli said. "It is unjustified. It's less than one half the length of the crook each of us holds. You're now flat on your back, and you may wave your sword around if you wish, but with a word from me, Asher and Aaron will use their staves to snap your neck like a street hen's. Our branches, as you call them, are quite robust, easily as hearty as your shinbones or spine, and your skull would split with a single blow."

"No matter to you," Ogen said, "my men will take care of the few of you, and the baby too."

Eli pressed his staff more insistently into Ogen's groin. "Much more from you and your best son will be nothing but a dream."

Ogen squirmed. He rested his sword on the ground but kept his grip.

Caleb said, "You won't be the first man who mistook the shepherd for the sheep. You may be surprised to learn that we carry knives. Even young Tobias here." Tobias pulled his tunic aside, revealing a knife handle.

"Look at my wrap," Eli said. The skin was shaggy in places and smooth elsewhere. "We guard the sheep of wealthy men. We are hard men tending soft mutton. I personally killed the wolf whose skin I wear with the very knife Tobias now uses and the staff that's even now about to disappoint the ladies of Jerusalem." He gave Ogen's genitals another poke.

"Your crooks could be ten cubits long," Ogen said. "My men and their swords will finish the five of you and this family and these useless star men in no time. You won't take them by surprise as you took me."

"Look over the wall," Caleb said.

Several dozen staves belonging to as many men and boys bristled above the stone fence of the stable. They waited their turn to enter the cave to worship the baby to which the brilliant song and Star had called them. They began to come forward on hearing Eli's stern tone and seeing an armed soldier upended. More were approaching from the street.

Eli laughed. "You're the fool, whatever your name is. The men you're looking at would beat you and your friends into hyena food in less than a minute."

There was an indistinct commotion outside where Ogen had left his soldiers. "Hear that! My men are already engaging your sheep men."

The shepherds snickered. "Apparently you've never heard a game of dice by moonlight with sheep men," Caleb said. "When we let you go, if we let you go, you'll find that some of my fellows have indeed engaged some of your brave soldiers, and more than likely relieved some of them of their armor and perhaps even a weapon or two, if my friend Uri happened to be carrying his special dice with him. In any event, you'll find little respect for Herod's guard here, and should you or your men be so foolish as to continue your threat against this family –"

"Please do not kill him," Mary said. "We do not want any kill—"

Joseph placed his hand on Mary's shoulder. "If for any reason the threat from this man and his companions should revive, we'll be grateful for any action you may take to preserve the life of the son of God."

"Without restraint or limit," he added.

Mary looked up at Joseph with surprise, and some pleasure, at his sudden assertion of leadership in their new little family.

"Let it be," she said.

"Asher, Aaron," Eli spoke to the two older boys with

their crooks around Ogen's neck. "Do not kill him just yet, but show our friend on the ground here how one might use a pair of poor shepherd's crooks to reduce his breath." Each boy pulled slowly on his staff until Ogen gasped and his eyes grew large. "Enough. Your sword, now," he said, and Ogen released it. "You and I and some of my fellows you see in the stable here will go see your companions and send you on your way."

Melchior spoke to Ogen: "Leave us our horses to ride and two donkeys for our packs. Take Herod's gold back to Herod."

"There was never any gold, you fool! None of you seers foresaw a thing!"

"Tell Herod what you will, if Herod even reigns," Melchior said. Tell him his brave guards fled beneath a laughing Star, and that you dropped your sword while your *shofka* shriveled at the end of a shepherd's stick."

"And if Herod is dead or deposed – God save you," Old Caspar said.

"And Ogen," Joseph said, "watch out for robbers. You would probably best them, as they are unlikely to be armed with shepherd's crooks."

Mary looked back at him with disapproval at the provocation, but the shepherds all laughed.

✧

"Tobias," Mary said.

She noticed that the boy had scarcely taken his eyes off Jesus even during the confrontation with Ogen. Eli and

Caleb and the two older boys had left him in the cave when they left to bid the guard farewell.

"Come over to me," she said.

He shuffled to Mary, who was holding Jesus and rocking gently in one of the chairs the men had made from the tavern's scraps.

"Would you like to hold him?"

"I have only held lambs," he said.

"This is the same, he is a lamb," Mary said. "You make a cradle with your arms. You will know what to do. You won't drop him. Nobody drops babies."

"I am not clean."

Mary laughed. "An hour ago he was inside my body, like the lambs you deliver from the ewes. And he is all wrapped up."

Joseph rose from his own chair. "Sit here. You'll feel more secure."

Joseph took Jesus from Mary and bent to Tobias. "See, your arms knew just what to do," he said.

Jesus blew some spit bubbles and his backside made a sound that made Tobias smile. Jesus, too.

"I'll pretend he's my brother," Tobias said.

"He's born to be brother to all of us," Mary said. "You will understand that someday."

Tobias nodded as he found himself rocking Jesus, their eyes joined.

I understand it now.

CHAPTER 26

Gifts

ELI AND CALEB recruited a group of larger and more unpleasant-looking shepherds to accompany them as they escorted Ogen to the far end of the stable where the soldiers and attendants were waiting. They made sure Ogen saw that most of the shepherds had knives, some more than one, in addition to their staves, although Eli told them to keep the cutlery out of sight so the guard would not be provoked. It was enough that Ogen knew.

While Ogen had been experiencing the hospitality of the cave, a senior captain had observed the sheep men's lopsided successes at dice and put a stop to those games before too many coins changed hands or any blood was shed. Two of the younger soldiers came up to Ogen and whispered angrily into his ear, but he shook his head and waved them away. The shepherds' winnings would stay won.

While the shepherds stood unsmilingly by, Ogen put a good face on things – Jerusalem tonight! There were cheers, but they were cheerless. A couple of the more seasoned soldiers noticed redness around Ogen's neck and dirt on the back of his armor. They did not recall his scabbard being empty when Melchior had fetched him forcibly down the alley to the cave. Still, there was no interest among the guard to question the order to turn around a third time in an hour. No one wished to risk his skull for the sake of those star men. They had not even returned with Ogen.

The guard had not unpacked anything in Ogen's absence; they turned the animals around and walked out more briskly than they had walked in. Ogen ordered silence until they were clear of the town.

∽

After Herod's guard was made to perceive the wisdom of returning to Jerusalem without the astrologers, the shepherds who had gathered took turns visiting Jesus, many kneeling at the tiny wooden manger, some weeping, all expressing their good wishes for the family. Jesus tipped between sleeping and waking, undisturbed at the attention and patient for Mary's breast. After the last of the shepherds had their turn at his bed, they returned to the hills to gather their flocks.

"I must say," Melchior said, "after the events of this night, and being in the presence of a guest of honor who spends most of his time suckling and burping and sleeping, it's difficult to know the direction the conversation should take."

"My own head is spinning," Balthazar said. "I can scarcely believe the honor, the gift, to which our journey has brought us."

"The honor is ours," Joseph said.

"Yes," Mary said. "We never doubted God's message to us, but –" She paused, as though saying anything would suggest just such doubt.

"But our being here, and the shepherds, too, is evidence and fulfillment of the prophecies," Old Caspar said, "and the beginning of God's message to the world beyond this stable."

"And so also with Sandar," Joseph said. "And Susannah."

"Everyone," Mary said.

She took a breath to say more but it caught in her throat, and for the first time since their journey from Nazareth began, Mary was entirely overcome. The months of her confinement, the long journey from Galilee, the drama of the final day and night, and her delivery of Jesus, all borne with stoicism and restraint, came together in her heart and she wept wordlessly and without shame.

Joseph knelt beside her, joined by Balthazar.

Old Caspar whispered to Melchior, "Who is Susannah?"

"I'm sorry," Mary said. "These are truly tears of joy and thanks." She paused. "And . . . relief, may God forgive me."

"You need not explain your tears to us," Old Caspar said. "We men know little of the winds that blow through a woman's heart."

"God knows," Balthazar said.

"God may," Old Caspar said, "or may not." He laughed. "I don't believe you've known enough women in your young life."

"Or perhaps too many gods," Melchior said.

"Susannah . . . ," Old Caspar said.

"Betrothed of Sandar," Joseph said, "and a midwife to Mary."

"He told us he had business in Jerusalem," Balthazar mused. "I would not have thought it was woman business."

"She proved an angel," Joseph said. "But she stole the devil's own voice to frighten away robbers on the road from Jerusalem."

"So Sandar acquired a wife since we saw him last night in Jericho," Melchior said.

"He did," Joseph said. "A striking woman, tall and fair, of high spirits and courage, and well suited to him."

"Sandar the Builder goes to town and comes back with a beauty," Old Caspar chuckled. "And they call *us* wise men."

∽

Balthazar said, "Gentlemen, the southlands beckon us. There is only one task left to us."

The others nodded. Now that things had quieted, the meaning of what they had seen and heard had begun to move through them.

Old Caspar dabbed at his eyes with the hem of his tunic. "My witness here today is greater than any reward I have received from reading the silent stars or the other unreliable signs our poor imaginings impose upon nature. To be here now, in this cave – I am bathed in riches."

"I'm not a man who struggles with words," Melchior said, "but tonight . . . ." He wiped away a tear.

There would be time for words.

"What is that aroma?" Mary said. "It's most pleasant in this home of the goat and the pig."

Balthazar was crumbling a nugget into a golden powder over one of the oil-lamp flames.

"Frankincense," he said.

CHAPTER 27

The Animals

A PAIR OF eyes watched from the underbrush as the guard passed by, now noisy and relieved that the strange search Herod had sent them on had ended. Some were arguing, some laughing, as they shuffled north on the road to Jerusalem.

The eyes could see that the donkeys and camels were tired. They didn't blink as they watched the company move down the road and disappear over a small rise. It was not long before the yelling and laughing could no longer be heard.

The moon was past its highest; the morning would come soon.

The Fox stepped onto the roadway and sat. He licked his nose and looked around. He settled and looked into the sky, north, toward the Pole Star.

There was a disturbance in the brush. The Lion emerged

from the roadside weeds and sat next to the Fox. He too looked into the northern sky.

They sat with their Fox and Lion thoughts.

Neither noticed that the little Frog had leapt into the scene. She croaked once to let them know she had arrived. Frogs can only jump and sit, so when she was done jumping she sat next to the Lion. She had no neck and could not face the sky, but she could still see the Pole Star with her Frog eyes.

The peace of this gathering was interrupted by the arrival of the Heron on the opposite roadside. He flapped noisily to a careful landing and stood there, his needle beak nipping at whatever was itching beneath his wing. His unattractive hacking sound *gaak* did not help his case for welcome with the others. He kept his distance, ready to take off if matters grew contentious, as he studied the trio lined up on the road.

The Lion inclined his head to the Fox.

He was of Herod.

The Fox kept his eyes on the northern sky.

He was. But he is of the story.

The Frog croaked again.

The Lion turned his face to the Heron. He slowly closed his eyes and opened them, once.

The Heron strode slowly over and stood next to the Frog.

The four animals faced the northern sky together.

On another day, another night, the Fox would fear the Lion, and the Frog the Heron, but this day and night they were free of their instincts and fears.

The Pole Star continued its slow circle of due north. The animals stood together until the sky began to purple, when, one by one, they returned to the wilderness.

The Pole Star

THE MOON HAD crossed the meridian. It was high enough in the southwestern sky to light the earth in a suggestive dream of morning to come.

Sandar and Susannah watched from above on Zac and Hannah as the shepherds returned to their fields, gathering in small groups to talk animatedly among themselves before dispersing to gather the wandering flocks. They could see Herod's guard and its retainers headed away from Bethlehem. They were too high to make out what was being said, but they could see knots of men yelling and gesturing as they rode back north on the Jerusalem road.

"Herod's men are slinking back to Jerusalem," Sandar said. "No horses, no magi. I wonder what happened in that cave."

Susannah said, "Every miracle of this day and night has protected and proclaimed the life of that baby. God did not leave that cave when we did."

Zac and Hannah began to pick up speed as they headed north.

"We were both part of many miracles today," Susannah said. "Now what?"

"I don't know," Sandar said. "Zac and Hannah have picked up the pace after we left the sky over the stable, and we're covering a fair piece of the countryside now. And as I think about it, other than to Nazareth with you, I have nowhere to go and am in no hurry to get there. Good thing, too; I wouldn't know where to guide them, or how, from this great height."

"Nowhere to go? I would suggest the ground."

"That would be ideal, my betrothed," Sandar said. "But Zac and I have no experience in navigating the sky, and I'm reluctant to experiment with what might happen if I erred with a command or the bridle."

"Well," she said, "we can't stay up here forever. While we may have participated in miracles, surviving with a lack of food and water and sleep and anything at all to do up here serves no miracle at all."

Sandar was silent. The donkeys and their riders continued to move swiftly through the air high above the hill country. Zac seemed incurious about his master's needs, following some voice that spoke only to him, and Hannah kept up alongside.

"I'm sorry, Susannah," he said. "I didn't lure you from the house of Nathan to drift forever over our land to no purpose. I expected, and I still expect, to make a life with you in Nazareth, with our children, God willing, but the purpose to which we have been called this night . . . I don't know how it's to be completed. There would seem to be nothing left for us in which to assist."

"Do you think we'll see Jesus again?" Susannah said. "Or Mary or Joseph?"

Sandar said, "So much seems new to me now, it's difficult even to know what the next hour will bring, the next sunrise."

"Mary spoke of our destiny," Susannah said. "I thought she meant our guidance of the shepherds and the magi. But she said we would have the love of children. Many children." She squeezed Sandar's arm.

"She did," Sandar said. "She said it to me earlier in the day on the road from Jericho as well."

"What is that village below us?" Susannah said.

Even in the moonlight Sandar recognized the patterns of his home town. "That's Nazareth. We've moved more swiftly than I thought. I can see our home from here."

"I like the sound of that, 'our home,'" Susannah said.

"I like the music in those words as well."

"Maybe we can persuade Zac and Hannah to drop us off there."

"Let's not use the word 'drop,' my betrothed. Zac has his head and is taking us where he will without guidance from me. Your Hannah seems content to join him."

The moonlit ground was becoming a blur as the donkeys flew ever faster. The few clouds approached and receded as the pair raced through the sky.

"What's that star?" Susannah said. "Zac has been headed in its direction since we showed the way to the shepherds and the magi. It's the only bright star in that part of the sky."

"They call it the Pole Star," Sandar said. "It circles true north as the night hours pass."

"What's north, other than Northmen and cold?"

"I wish I knew," Sandar said. "But Zac, or whatever — may I say angel? – is guiding him seems to think it's a good idea to go there, and your Hannah doesn't object. Maybe they believe it to be the home of more flying livestock."

"So perhaps more miracles await us north?"

"I expect so," Sandar said. "God has provided for his helpers this day and I'm sure we won't be forsaken in whatever this journey turns out to be. I do find myself hoping they're warm miracles." He pulled a sheepskin from his pack and draped it around Susannah's shoulders. He recalled the fine bright red blanket trimmed in white he had fancied during their visit to the merchants in Jerusalem and found it among the items they had assembled before their departure from the market. He pulled it close around him against the chill.

Sandar pulled the wood toy in the shape of Zac from the folds of his wrap. He held it up to examine it more closely in the moonlight, considering ways he might smooth it out for a little one's grasp, or perhaps make a new one whose moving limbs and head would provoke a child's laughter and imagination.

"I forgot to leave the toy for Jesus," he said.

"It's a sign you're destined to return," Susannah said. "Perhaps on his birthday."

Susannah and Sandar had a sudden understanding that

the world before them was truly new, and they kissed, the Pole Star rising slowly ahead of them. "Tied to a home," Susannah said. "Another old way we may reconsider."

"Joseph was right," Sandar said. "Everything changed tonight."

Zac and Hannah raced into the darkness, a heaven newly connected to the earth.

Susannah leaned over and patted Sandar's belly. "Sandar, called the Builder," Susannah said, "you are far too lean to bear the winds of the north. We'll need to fatten you up against the cold like the sheep of the fields."

She ran her hand over the fleecy white stubble that had begun to appear on his cheeks.

"Your face is likewise unguarded," she said. "I think you should grow a beard."

Sandar laughed, quietly as first, more heartily as he considered Susannah's suggestions, and as he felt the sky rushing past he was filled with an inspired, ecstatic joy, and he threw his head back and laughed louder and his cap flew off and his white hair was thick with waves and crazy with the breeze and his face shone ruddy, and the Spirits were with them and he knew his destiny and he laughed a new laugh, deeply and truly, over and over, *ho ho ho*.

END

Made in the USA
Las Vegas, NV
30 November 2022